LADY SHADE

YMIR A. LETHE

This book is dedicated to Rhiannon
The person who reminded me people are worth fighting for.
The greatest friend I could hope to have.

NOTE FROM THE AUTHOR

The tale of Lady Shade is a mystery. This mystery, however, doesn't end with the murder at the beginning or with the beast that stalks the town of Bronzeglade. It spans every facet of every character's mind.

The line between truth and fiction has always been thin, and the human mind isn't as good at making this distinction as we think. This book will explore this divide through the lens of a gothic murder mystery, and I hope it will fascinate and intrigue you.

I also think it's important to remember the legend of the lycanthrope—the beast in the woods that lived a double life as a friendly human face in the village. Never forget the old stories. They reveal all.

ACT 1

BYRON PORTSMAN

THE INNKEEPER

THE WHITE HART INN WAS A QUIET LITTLE THING OWNED BY A large man who only loved his hotel, his daughter, and his dearly departed wife. So even though the White Hart Inn stood on the edge of the small town square and only lodged pilgrims who came to visit the old monastery in the forest, he took care with all things.

The sunlight, which had to angle through the windows past the high rooftops and great spire of the church opposite, gleamed off of pristine furnishings. The bar and dining area was perfectly kept with a warm fire. The logs to fuel it were slick oak from the Bronzeglade forest. Every tanker and glass was immaculate and filled with only the best.

The Inn only had a few guests. It was autumn which meant it was full harvest, so the men and women of the rural lands were hard at work. But Mr. Portsman, the innkeeper, had one guest who was unlike any he'd seen. Out here, it was unimaginable that a woman would be in riding leathers and roll into town on a black stallion, but there she was. Her fiery hair draped around her face, which was covered in makeup that accentuated her cheekbones and made her blue eyes shine brighter. She had an intelligent glint in her eye, and her boots were up on the chair beside her as she drank a tankard of ale.

Mr. Portsman could tell she was a city type, and from what little she had said to him, he learned that she was part of London's aristocracy, here to see the local lord. She had a weapon strapped to her side that was far too complex and for Mr. Portsman to recognize, but she'd explained that it was called a wheel-lock pistol and that it worked similar to a crossbow. Her last name, Shade, was apparently the name of a great line of generals who'd fought in many wars. And her father had named her Milla, after a lady he'd met while fighting over in France. It seemed fitting. A wayward heart in two ways.

His only other guest was a pagan man who spent most of his time out in the forest. The pilgrims at the old monastery said they often saw him wandering the barren halls, reading the old books which had survived the fire that scorched half the monastery. He was said to be a shaman, and inquisitors had come looking for him a couple times, but the man never stayed in town very long. He wore a black shroud, bone-charms, and rings with strange gems in them. His black hair mostly covered his face.

The man said his name was Solace, but no one in the town or any nearby knew where he'd come from. It was even suggested that he could be some kind of spirit. But Solace appeared entirely human to Mr. Portsman as he sat there drinking an ale of his own, uninterested in the striking lady beside him.

Mr. Portsman finished cleaning the table and nodded to Solace. "How long you staying?"

"Not too long, I hope." Solace set down his tankard. "I just need to ask Father Blossom for some help with my research."

Milla put down her tanker.

"What are you researching? And do either of you want more ale?"

Milla shook her head and took another sip. Solace gestured with the empty cup and Mr. Portsman took it, then strolled over to the bar. He turned the tap and looked at Solace.

"A bit of history," he said. "Do you remember when I left for a year?"

"I do." Mr. Portsman nodded. "They came looking for you twice."

"Well, amusingly, I went to Rome. Turns out, the monastery here wasn't built by the Catholic Church. A miracle of God, they say. I'm interested in learning where it came from."

"That is interesting." Mr. Portsman handed Solace a full cup. "But there are more serious matters. What about the murder in the forest?"

"What about it?" Solace asked. "The Bronzeglade is massive. You townspeople sometimes forget it extends far beyond the reaches of known lands. Doesn't surprise me a pack of wolves would venture out every now and then."

"Not from what I've heard," Mr. Portsman said. "It would've needed to be a big wolf."

"Perhaps it was," Milla said.

Both men gave her a curious glance. She sat the cup at the end of the table

"More ale?" Mr. Portsman refilled her tanker.

"You know," Solace said, "there've been tales for about a hundred years of beasts possessed by demons. Whether by the denizens of the shadows or from what you call Satan, there are stories of men whose minds become that of a wolf. That we know is true. And from what I've heard, the body can follow."

There was silence.

"Superstitious nonsense." Milla smirked as Mr. Portsman returned her cup to her.

"Pardon?" Solace said.

"I've heard a great many tales, and none of them are true," Milla said. "Vampires and werewolves and witches—please. Nothing could hope to challenge the Father above."

"I didn't take you for a believer," Solace said. "Wearing—"

"Times are changing, and so is the Faith," Milla said. "Here up north, you're still Catholic. In London, it swings this way and that, and the madness of it all has killed thousands. No, I won't subject myself to such nonsense."

"So which are you?" Mr. Portsman asked.

"I'm a follower of the Lord." Milla gulped from the tankard. "It's interesting about the monastery, though. You know, the early Romans built some primitive monasteries. They could've built it, monks moved in, fixed it up, built more. Makes the most sense to me."

Solace grinned. "Don't think you're the only educated one here, Miss Shade."

"How do you know my last name?" Milla asked.

"I must be on my way." Solace stood. "It's always wonderful, Mr. Portsman. And I think you'll be the woman Eratta needs. Someone to fire up his soul, which became cinders when his leg began to wither. Good day."

Milla drew her pistol on Solace. "Don't walk away. How do you know my last name?"

"Come find me and I'll tell you more. But this is a place of light." Solace gestured to the windows. "And of ears. Certainly not a place to talk about dark things."

"You're doing it again," Mr. Portsman said.

"Oh, I'm not doing that!" Solace laughed, slapping the innkeeper on the shoulder. "I'll perform rituals of good health for you and your daughter, and put flowers of comfort by your wife's resting place. Miss Shade, take good care of yourself. And if you're ever in need of silver, ask Nathaniel. His family owns the silver mine up in the grey hills."

Solace skipped out the front and headed to the market. Milla watched him exchange a few friendly words, buy a fresh baked pie and some fruit, and go on his way. She put the pistol back in its holster and groaned, slumping back onto her seat, then guzzled down her ale.

"Excuse him," Mr. Portsman said. "They say he's got a demon in his head."

"We've all got demons in our head, because that's what the snake of Eden made us, is it not?"

"You're as bad as him!" Mr. Portsman laughed, slapping his hand on his bar. "Have you met Sir Winters yet?"

"No. And we're not arranged—he's just a suitor. I must admit, I am rather... rebellious for a lady. I need a man who doesn't bore me."

"You're lucky you're from such a well-off family, but I think Eratta is far from boring."

"No one thinks their local lord is boring." Milla shrugged. "Trust me, they can be incredibly boring."

"Well, luck to you." Mr. Portsman gave a firm nod. "I've got to make sure my daughter is doing her reading."

"Teaching her to read and write? Smart man. The printing press—"

"What?"

"They've found a way to make machines write. Well, write what's already been written. So reading and writing will be incredibly valuable one day soon. I'll take myself to bed."

"I haven't given you the key yet. I'll sort the room to ensure all the bedding is in place, and take your bags up for you. Father Blossom should be returning from his duties by now, if you still want to talk with him."

"Oh, thank you." Milla smiled and gave a skirtless curtsey, then strolled out the front door, toward the church.

Mr. Portsman finished off the rest of her half-empty cup, then cleaned it. He was smiling, with an arched brow. Solace had known far too much about that lady, and that talk of wolves seemed more like a threat than proper conversation. He'd have to talk with Nathaniel in the morning.

Mr. Portsman climbed the staircase and peered into his daughter's bedroom to see that she was reading. He beamed, then closed the door and went about making sure Lady Shade's room was in order. He carried up her bags, sorted the bedding, cleaned the mirror, and dusted the ornate wooden floor, walls, and rafters. He opened the windows at the right angle to give the perfect view over town. Checked to make sure the drawers of the bedside table, dresser, and wardrobe were empty, and ensured that the wooden plank walls were firm by knocking twice on each, before finally setting her bags on the bed and then heading downstairs.

"Just the keys and the horse now." He found the keys enough in his bedside drawer, and strolled into his yard.

The moonlight gleamed in the night sky.

He went to the stable, checked the hay and the water, then admired Milla's stallion. A massive, beautiful creature, well-bred and well-trained.

"All right," Mr. Portsman stepped out into the courtyard and looked across.

He saw something familiar in the shadows. Green-Eyes—an enormous beast covered in white fur, with a body like that of a goliath. His back arched above the tall wooden fencing of the yard. Claws were long and he stood like an ape, his knuckles grazing the grass.

"I had to send her on her way," Mr. Portsman shrugged, "because I knew you'd come."

It didn't respond.

"I got no clue where he's staying. I'd say try the monastery again."

The lycanthrope rose its chest and crouched its legs, arched its neck toward the star-filled sky, then leaped for the rooftop. It charged over several buildings and out of sight. Mr. Portsman returned home. All this talk of wolves, but Green-Eyes had never killed anyone, so Mr. Portsman wondered, if not him, who had killed that poor woman?

TUBIEL HASS

THE EXILED INQUISITOR

THE TOWN OF BRONZEGLADE WOULD'VE MADE A GREAT painting. From the church, rolled the town and its fields of golden wheat.

Tubiel had found his favorite spot on the hillside, on top of a giant rock where the church spire cut between the two grey hills behind it. The chill autumn wind blew through his hair and ran over his face, and he couldn't help but smile. He looked to the open sky and saw white clouds coming over the mountains, but he could still see the sun.

"Thank you, Lord for such a beautiful place."

Tubiel jerked his head to the source of a spout of noise. Eight militiamen were marching up the road, toward him. He remembered that one had wound up to Heron's Mound, a pagan burial site, so he jumped off the rock and closed his purple robes.

"Sirs, what's happened?" he yelled.

The captain paused to look at him before proceeding without a word. Captain Daniel had fought in the king's army, against rebellious Scots just north of the border. He was tall and lean now, rather than the hulking warrior he had been.

9

Tubiel followed the militia as they advanced over the hill, to Heron's Mound. It was a giant stone circle pieced together with enormous hewn stone and seven pillars in the center. The rocks that had once created a mound in the center were now scattered, revealing the burial ground's entrance. He walked up to the mound and joined the militiamen as they peered down the staircase, which led into darkness.

Captain Daniel ran his hand through his short brown hair, glancing at the soldiers. Then he inspected at the ground until Tubiel tapped him on the shoulder.

"I'll go," Tubiel said.

"Not you, holy man," Daniel said. "I'll go."

Tubiel nodded. "Very well."

Daniel began his descent into the tomb, and returned after a few minutes. He brushed off the dust that now coated him and looked at the new arrival—Solace the pagan, Tubiel just saw him once Daniel noticed him. Tubiel glared at the shaman, who gave him a queer smile. Tubiel dropped his hand to his side, where his mace was hidden beneath his robes, but he knew better than to try anything with the pagan. He alone couldn't take on whatever demon lived inside that man.

"Anything in there?" Solace asked.

"No," Daniel said. "It's an old burial ground. Holes in the walls stuffed with dead bodies. They only treated one with any kind of respect."

"Only one?"

"Yeah, it was in a giant stone box. Didn't notice anything."

"Tubiel, you're a smart man," Solace said. "And we're both educated. I'll take a look, as an expert on all things old."

Daniel thought for a moment and nodded.

"I'm not going down there with that demon," Tubiel said.

"I'm not a demon. I'm but a mortal man!" Solace bowed and then entered the darkness of Heron's Mound.

Tubiel looked around at the militiamen, who were busy searching for clues as to who'd disturbed the tomb, and finally decided to follow Solace into the tomb. The stone was smooth and the sunlight gleamed off of the walls all the way down the spiral staircase, into the massive box tomb. Daniel had already taken the lid off, and Solace was analyzing the body.

"Danish," he said. "Which means these weren't Danish, or they'd have cremated them."

Tubiel looked at the writing and realized Solace was right. Then he also inspected the body, which was caked in dust.

"A ring was stolen," Tubiel said.

Solace looked to the skeleton. "You're right." He lifted the skeleton's arm and inspected the finger, which was dust-free. "You can see where the bone had warped inward from growing with the ring on. Family heirloom, probably."

"All this to steal one ring." Tubiel shook his head. "But why bury these people? Surely they'd have thrown them in a river if they didn't respect them."

"I don't know, but we have to put the stones back. We can both agree that the dead should be kept resting."

"Agreed."

Tubiel noticed something on Solace's hand. The only jewelry not made of twig or bone. A simple silver ring with a gleaming blue stone. Solace followed Tubiel's gaze to his hand, and Tubiel dropped his hand to the shaft of his mace on his hip.

"This is my ring." Solace lifted his hand to display the ring. "See? Fits perfectly."

Tubiel sneered before looking over the runes. "Can you read what they say?"

"I'm a bit rusty. I think the man buried here was meant to be a god-chieftain. I keep seeing something similar to *jarl*, but that's not quite right."

"Where did you get that ring?"

"It was my mother's father's." Solace turned and looked him in the eye. "Stop. We've got a robbery of a sacred place and you're busy making accusations, simply because you don't like me."

Tubiel stared back into Solace's creepy orange eyes, with a huff and curled his lower lip. Then he stormed up the stone staircase and back into the sunlight. Two new people had arrived. On the left was a lady in a tight red dress, with long fiery hair. And on the right was the local priest, Father Blossom. He was a young man, likeable, too. The lady peered into the darkness, while the priest was asking questions.

"Who's she?" Tubiel asked Father Blossom, gesturing to the lady.

"I'm Lady Milla Shade," she said. "Here visiting Lord Winters."

"My apologies." Tubiel bowed. "Daniel, we should re-seal the tomb. It was robbed, and now we leave the dead to rest."

Solace emerged from the staircase brushing the dust from his black fur cloak. "Agreed!"

"Seems right." Daniel nodded. "Marcon, go and find Nathaniel. Tell him to send a few laborers to help us move these rocks."

The militiaman nodded and began jogging for the hills.

"The rocks weren't just toppled," Milla said. "There was a lot of force used."

"Would've taken a giant," Tubiel said. "Or ropes."

Milla turned to Father Blossom. "Well, thank you, Father." She smiled. "I don't know what I'd have done without you."

"No problem. Sorry I wasn't there when you came to visit. Byron should know by now that I spend a lot of the evening gathering medicinals." Blossom sighed. "And it's getting harder to find quality as winter comes."

"Why would he send me during that time?" Milla asked.

"I don't know." Father Blossom shrugged. "He was probably tired. He's a hard-working man, that Mr. Portsman. Tubiel, how are you?"

Lady Shade began walking off.

"I'm good," Tubiel said.

Tubiel looked in her direction. "She's an interesting figure."

She stopped to glare at him and then carried on.

She's a beautiful lady, and with a thick London accent. A sharp mind also. A little rude, though. Tubiel returned his attention to Father Blossom to find that he'd already begun talking with one of the militiamen. Eventually, Father Blossom bowed and left without another word.

Prick. Tubiel sighed before deciding to go on his way. Back over the hill and up another grassy slope to the forest, he found the cabin that was his home. He watered the plants, checked the irrigation which ran from the nearby river that divided the east side of the Bronzeglade forest in half, and then entered his cabin. He went to his desk in the corner, sat down, and looked through his papers. No reference to a ring or anything.

"Who are you?" He held up his sketch of Solace, and made a popping noise with his tongue. "No, you're not the green-eyed wolf. But perhaps you know who is."

Green-Eyes had been sighted for the last ten years, but not a single killing yet. It seemed that he kept to itself. So what could've possibly killed the poor woman on the road?

A second wolf.

The sun was setting and the sky was drenched in red. He looked out of his open door and smiled to himself. The Lord put many annoying things in this world, but he also made sunsets.

Tubiel looked through his notes. The mysterious Monastery of Bronzium, with an unknown origin. No architect, not even a sect attached to it. Endless historical documents and religious reading. Nothing special about the place except that it was heretical.

Tubiel froze. Felt like something was right outside his door, watching him. He jumped to his feet and ran to the door. Looked out through the bleak trees and saw someone standing far away, in the darkness. Silence hung like fog. It was too dark to see who they were. He couldn't even make out their outline. He just knew they were there, and he knew they were watching.

"Solace? Is that you?"

The bleeding red sky began to fade into black. Tubiel touched his wrist and felt the chill of his silver bracelet as the dark figure slipped back into the darkness to reveal a full moon, through silver oak and drifting black leaves. Tubiel reached into his robes and pulled out mace. When he looked up, fiery eyes blazed through the darkness.

"A demon lives within you, lycanthrope!"

The black-furred beast leaped and landed a dozen feet away from him, on the verge between the trees and the open ground. Its fur opened in places, and the flesh soon after, from which fire flared into trails. Its teeth were shrouded in black smoke, and its eyes burned.

"The second wolf," Tubiel snarled.

The two stepped toward one another. The beast writhed as its head was knocked aside with a mace, and then he kicked the lycanthrope onto its back. The beast rolled back onto its belly and glared at Tubiel, growling.

"This is a silver mace," Tubiel said.

The beast didn't even flinch.

"Fuck, you're far gone, aren't you? A young one, I see!"

It leaped for him again and Tubiel ducked beneath it.

He'd faced many of these beasts, and he knew the beasts who'd only recently turned. They were wild and unfocused, and though they were strong, they didn't compare to the older Lycans.

It turned its head and tried to bite his throat, but Tubiel swung between the hinges of its jaw and it bit clean through the silver. It shrieked, thrashing its head and throwing shards of silver everywhere. It spewed blood from its mouth as it staggered further and further back from Tubiel before falling against a tree, still staring at Tubiel. It started spewing less and less blood, and the fire that enveloped it was growing.

Tubiel looked to the shattered hilt of the mace and swore as the beast began to get up. Angry, savage. Even if Tubiel escaped, this thing could start a forest fire if they fought any longer. He sighed and whispered to God, then ripped his silver bracelets free. The fiery beast lunged toward him and Tubiel bellowed a howl which rolled through the trees, and swiped the underside of its jaw, snapping its head back. The beast rolled and looked up at its adversary, which now controlled Tubiel's mind. The golden wolf bared its fangs.

Tubiel gasped, barged through the door of his house and took one stride across the room before collapsing. His body seized and shuddered in the sunlight. The wounds had sealed. The burn marks had vanished, but his body was consumed with pain.

ERATTA WINTERS

LORD OF THE BRONZEGLADE

Eratta's home was of his father's making. Its enormous walls were made of stone bricks, with stone guard towers. His withered right leg had begun feeling much better, thanks to Nathaniel learning some new skills during his trip to York, and Errata's walk along the perimeter was like a trip down memory lane.

Jorvan Winters, a Danish mercenary who'd fallen into favor with King Henry VIII in the field of battle in France, had been a good father to Eratta. Even when he proved to be less of a warrior than his father, Jorvan loved him unconditionally. Eratta's mother had died in childbirth, and Eratta was sad that his father had died believing his son would go off to war. That was a year before his leg began to wither and Eratta was put on a boat straight back to England. His father had succumbed to madness before these was were built, and died when he went out into the forest. They found him a week later at the White Falls. He'd thrown himself off the top.

Eratta gave a sad smile as he remembered his father before the mania had consumed him, and took out his pocket watch. Miss Shade would be arriving to meet him shortly, so he grabbed his crutch and limped back around the walls, toward his gardens which contained patches of assorted colored flowers and fountains that irrigated the long rows of hedges, all planned by Eratta. He arrived at the front steps of his manor, where two of his servants stood waiting.

"Tell Hork to begin making the dinner," Eratta said. "Inform Nathaniel that Miss Shade will be arriving shortly, and I'll want the doors leading to the drawing room and to the dining room already open."

The servants hurried into the house. Eratta waited on the front step as the main gates were opened and Milla rode in on the back of a black stallion. He suppressed a chuckle of impressment and only smiled as she approached with Father Blossom at her side. He waved to Eratta, who raised his hand in return, before Blossom turned around and left.

Eratta was a striking figure with the pale skin of a Dane but the thin body of a Brit. His long white hair that fell to his shoulders. He liked to dress in reds and blues, and today he was wearing a noble blue coat with a high collar.

Milla dismounted once she got to the front of the gardens. "I love the gardens!" she called. "Sir Winters?"

"Call me Eratta, Miss Shade." He bowed. "Come into the drawing room. Do you drink?"

"Yes." She smiled. "And call me Milla."

"I shall." He nodded.

Nathaniel opened the door, from inside.

"That's my butler, Nathaniel." He nodded to his butler.

Nathaniel closed the door behind them and left to check on the kitchens. Eratta lead Milla up the staircase and into the drawing room, closed the door, and offered her a seat. She chose a different one, further from the window, and Eratta sat opposite.

"I like the black dress," he said. "Fits well."

"I don't. I like to wear riding leathers." Milla sighed. "Have you seen what's been going on in the town?"

"Well, I've been dealing with a string of robberies on the road and an animal attack in the forest, so a disturbed tombstone is the least of my concerns. But I'm going to personally visit Heron's Mound tomorrow."

"It's been covered up now." She shrugged. "What happened to your leg?"

"The muscles became weak and useless and died. Shame, too. I was considered a crack shot back then."

"Were you?" She grinned. "Not as good as me, I promise."

"I'll take you up on that. You're interesting. Ladies are usually—"

"Boring and weak? Yeah, I choose not to be. They ride small horses because it looks prettier. Guess who turns heads."

"That stallion." He smiled.

"And me!" She sat back in the armchair. "What are you lord of, anyway?"

"Only a few towns. But we export a lot of silver, so we're pretty well off. My father decided to mine the mountain, and got lucky. Your father was a Brigade general, right?"

"He was. He was knighted after proving himself on the field of battle." She beamed. "He's old now. Still speaks like a soldier, though."

"Did he teach his daughter to shoot?"

"No, I learned that in France. "I was a nurse. Found myself a rifle, taught myself to shoot. Came in handy, too, when our camp was attacked in a night raid."

"Kill anyone?"

"Three. Have you killed anyone?"

"Ordered people executed. Watched each of them die. I think that's what a pistol does, don't you?"

"I killed one of them with a tent pole." Milla sighed. "But I don't regret a thing. I think women are too weak."

"Weak? They hold homes upon their—"

"Men and women are weak in different ways. Women are weak of will. Men are weak of mind, and that's how it's always been.

Men, because they're too comfortable. Women, because they're scared."

"Hmm. Are you well-educated, Miss Shade?"

"In some things. Medicines, weapons, people, politics. I'm an only daughter, so my father has taught me well. Sir Shade cares about his legacy, apparently."

Eratta said nothing more and instead poured her a glass of whiskey. She smiled and nodded as she took it, then sipped at the drink while Eratta poured himself another. It was clear that Milla spent most of her time venturing away from home and using that she was from London to excuse her bad manners. But Eratta didn't care much for manners. Out here, all his friends were common folks he'd briefly served alongside during the war, before he was forced to return home, and his soldiers came with him.

"You're an interesting one," he said. "And beautiful, if you don't mind me saying."

"I don't."

"But I'd be interested in how you'd act at a ball party. You must understand, I'm wealthy. I don't show it off. I put most of my money into developing the town and the farmland. But it does mean that I go to social gatherings."

"I do just fine. Maybe drink a bit much, but I'm fine." She chuckled. Now I need to talk to you about something. I'm deeply concerned by what's happening in this town."

"It's no—"

"I'm from the Shade family. The last of them. And people seem to be forgetting their duty to deal with the demons that walk the earth."

He sat upright. "What are you—"

"The Shade family is a long line of werewolf hunters. "I'm in this town to meet you, but I couldn't help but notice you've turned a blind eye to the same beast that turned your father mad."

Eratta's eyes became hot with anger and he clenched the arm of the chair with his right hand. His chest and throat tightened.

She stared into his eyes. "You know I'm right."

He took a few moments to calm down. "The green-eyed wolf has only ever been the ravings of madmen. And you—a werewolf huntress? Lycanthropes don't even exist."

"Hmm... I've killed five." She grinned. "But of course they don't exist. Your father saw one, several people have witnessed it, but it isn't real. Surely."

"Suddenly, I like you less."

"I know. I'm a lady who doesn't take men's bullshit. Look, you're a likeable man, Eratta, and you've got a good heart. But as a huntress, the last of a long line, it's my job to make sure this wolf-demon is dealt with. Which means I'll tell you about it."

"I don't believe it, not one bit. You're mad!"

Milla looked out the window. The sun was setting and the open sky was turning red.

"I'm leaving." She huffed. "I hope you grow up between now and my return." She stormed out of the drawing room.

Eratta took several deep breaths before picking up his crutch and following after her. She had already exited out the side gate and was walking into the forest. He hobbled after her until he found her sitting on a log. She glared at him as he approached.

She'd picked a beautiful part of the glade to be angry in. The trees were turning orange, and the leaves blood-red as the sun set over them. Milla's bright orange hair looked soft and comforting, but her face was one of boiling anger. Her astounding beauty only made it more terrifying, like an angered dryad.

"You're risking the lives of the people in this town!" She sighed and the anger in her eyes faded. "I'll be along in a minute. Just go back inside."

"You know what, I'm going to look into this the best I can." He nodded. "Come on, let's eat."

Milla looked up as the sky began to fade from red to black. "I don't want to be alone out here anyway, with the beast about."

She started walking back inside, but paused and turned back towards the forest.

"What is it?" he asked.

"Something's coming. Go. I'll be right behind you."

Eratta hurried back inside.

A RELATED TALE

Forgive me if my writing is hard to read, but my hand won't stop shaking. I've been in and out of asylums for three years, with doctors telling me what I saw was either a trick of the devil or an affliction of the mind brought about by some sickness. But I've been through all the exorcisms and all the treatments a man's soul can bear, so I'll write what I saw and maybe then I may find clarity.

My name is David Far. For many years, I've been part of Her Majesty's Armed Forces and have fought in India and Africa. I was promoted to General after acts of valor and with the help my wealthy uncle. It was during my time in Africa that I saw what I saw. I had killed fourteen men with my rifle, ordered the execution of more, and killed a man in hand-to-hand combat.

Driven by sheer loyalty to Her Majesty, I led the front against an African warlord, in a jungle. This one was sharper-witted than his primitive brethren, and far more tenacious than me. Our force of ten thousand men was ambushed in the jungle and many of my soldiers were slaughtered, forcing us into a retreat. Most of my men got out alive, but I, like many others, were lost among the strange lands of giant trees and thick bush. I spent hours feeling like I would die from the humidity, and I spent hours with chattering teeth while fighting off hypothermia from the heavy rainfall. I ventured for days, my compass broken, looking for any place I could call shelter so that I could find my bearings. The thought of suicide crossed my mind several times over the next few days. I'd gone hungry before, but there was no hunger quite like I felt then.

Eventually, I managed to catch a monkey with a bullet and I cooked myself a meal. But I was left weak, and my mind was weak, too. The hunger, the pain, the weakness, the suffering—all that kept me going was knowing that if I died, my wife and child wouldn't be able to live full lives.

Finally, after days of venturing through that accursed jungle, I managed to find a great, tall stone structure. A relic of an ancient time, I supposed. It had been warded off by the natives, with totems and painted signs. Of course, I didn't pause for the superstitious beliefs of cannibals, believing there was only one greater power—God. So I found myself an overhang and had the first good night's sleep I'd had in weeks.

The structure was like the pyramids I'd heard of in Egypt and the southern Americas, but this one was made of a brownish stone and had three sheer sides. The other side was stepped with rings of carved rock. Using what few materials I could scavenge, I was able to paint a map upon the stone. I could see for miles around, and though I couldn't see out of the jungle, I could see landmarks. I was able to venture out to them and paint maps there, building each map greater and further. This carried on for about three days as I finally developed a routine of making the map, hunting, eating, sleeping. It seemed that I would eventually be able to return to civilization, and my mind finally began to return to me. I was calm and determined. I would return to my men and then to my family as soon as I could. As for the war, I was done. I would resign my position as General.

After returning from the furthest venture I had ever undertaken, I noticed a small detail in the pyramid that I hadn't noticed before. In the side opposite the steps, halfway up, there was a small black rectangle—a dark doorway to the interior of the structure—and I immediately went to investigate it. I wouldn't venture deep. I didn't know this place, and it's likely that the natives thought it dangerous because it was like a maze within. But when I stepped into the threshold of darkness, I found no labyrinth, no minotaur. Instead, it was a simple square room with bare walls, except a painting on the opposite wall. What confused me was that it was a beautiful depiction. A white man dressed in a long black shroud, with hair that fell down to his knees and long, sharp nails. He shared something with the natives —a bone necklace, the same wild look in his eyes. There was nothing else in this room and I thought nothing more of what I'd seen, not real- izing it was a dire warning.

The moment I left that chamber, I could feel the pale man's eyes watching my back, and they didn't go when I turned the corner. While I'd looked upon the image, I saw pristine beauty, maybe what the natives saw in their spirits. But now I could feel it, among the trees, in the darkness. It felt like something was watching. Not hungry. Not angry. Not even malicious. But observing and watching me, how I believed God looked down on me.

It was the day after that, a man I recognized emerged from the trees. I kept out of view, hiding in the overhang and watching him—the great warlord who had so terribly defeated me and my men. In his arms was a soldier of Her Majesty's legion, one of my men, barely breathing. Likely already a dead man, by all accounts. I loaded my rifle, *preparing to shoot him in the back. But as I loaded every round, I could feel the eyes grow angrier, so instead I returned to being an observer. I'm not subservient, but I knew I couldn't shoot that man.*

The warlord descended the steps, and as I watched him go I realized he had no soldier in his arms. The moment he was gone, I dashed up the steps to find the soldier lying with his back on the stone, looking up at the sun. He didn't look at me. My shadow fell over him and his gaze shifted to the tree line. I jerked around, thinking the warlord had come back, perhaps with some kind of sacrificial dagger. But I could no longer feel the eyes watching me.

Every ounce of strength and determination left my flesh, and I could only stare as he stepped from the trees. The most beautiful thing I've ever seen, with pale skin and long black claws. It was something between human and something not quite. The bones rattled around its neck, and its eyes seemed to burn with a smothered fire. All life had been snuffed out. Its naked, bony foot fell upon the lowest step and I looked down at the soldier, who was now looking up at the endless void that was the rest of God's creation. It got to the top of the steps and I noticed then that I was merely inches from it, so I snapped my rifle up and I took aim. It looked back at me and I became paralyzed again.

It wasn't scared or angry. It was interested. It reached out and grabbed the rifle from my hands, threw it down the side of the pyramid, and looked down at the soldier before shivering in a way that came with sexual pleasure. Lastly, it turned to me and moved closer, then whispered in my ear. Seven words, spoken like a spider spinning its silky web, and then I was lying with my back on the stone, looking up at a cold night's sky.

Seven unspeakable words I won't repeat. Words that tainted my heart and put something dark in my veins.

I would find my way out of the jungle, but I still felt that strange creature watching me, mocking me every moment. And now I know who I am, where I am, and the fate that awaits me. It isn't heaven or hell. I have no time for places of fiction.

No, I have a much stranger place waiting, past death.

SOLACE

THE PAGAN

It was a chilly night in Bronzeglade. Solace loved the forest during the day, when the trees were rich and brown and the leaves an entrancing bronze. But right now the bark was silver and the leaves black. A howl had rolled through the town from the Winters Estate, and Solace dashed in that direction. He stood on a verge which looked over the estate, his dark shroud wrapped around him, long-barreled rifle in his hands, and he was freezing.

He tapped the blue-stone ring against a rock beside him and hopped to his feet. Leaped from the rock and slid down the hillside, bracing his fall with the towering walls of the estate. He sniffed the air and smelled something foul.

"What the fuck are you doing here?"

Solace turned to see Tubiel standing by the estate's side gate, silver dagger in one hand and silver mace in the other, peering through the gateway into the gardens. Solace held a finger up to his lips and crept toward Tubiel.

"I'm guessing I wasn't the only one who heard the beast," Solace whispered.

"Yeah, it came from this way," Tubiel said. "All right, well, I know you're not one of them, at least."

Solace nodded toward the entrance. "Let's go in."

Tubiel opened the gate and let Solace to go first. Solace slipped through into the gardens, and hid behind one of the many low hedges at the front of the house. He could through the windows and into the dining room, where Milla and Eratta were eating.

"Check two, for not Lycans," Solace said.

"Hm." Tubiel crouched beside Solace. "Any sign?"

Solace peered through the darkness. "Yeah." He pointed to a room directly above the dining room.

It was dark, but he could make out a pair of gleaming eyes. The giant white beast smashed its paw through the glass, then leaped free and gripped the ledge. It swung around like an ape, kicked through the dining hall window and crashed against the table. Milla jumped to her feet, reaching under her dress, and pulled out a wheel-lock pistol. She fired a shot that slammed into the beast's chest. Solace took aim and shot it in the back. Eratta screamed and collapsed to the floor.

"Go," Solace hissed.

Tubiel nodded and they both dashed for the dining hall. The white-furred beast turned to the unexpected adversaries and roared. Then Milla loaded another bullet and shot the beast in the leg. It yelped, and as Tubiel vaulted over a hedge, the beast lunged to meet him. Tubiel sprayed it in the face with mace and slashed its wrist with his silver knife. The beast shrieked and stumbled backward, and Solace fired another round. Green-Eyes grabbed the table and toppled over it to put a barrier between him and his three enemies. Tubiel rushed in behind the table. He cursed when the dining room door crashed against the floor and the beast escaped. Solace loaded another round into his rifle.

"What is it doing here!" Eratta cried, as Milla helped him to his feet.

"It's hunting the huntress," Tubiel said.

Solace tracked Green-Eyes through the manor as it moved to higher levels. Solace moved back, into the gardens, keeping aim with his rifle at the place he guessed it would emerge. Milla, Eratta, and Tubiel climbed out of the window and joined him. Sure enough, it smashed through the glass roof of the conservatory and Solace fired. The shot blasted into the beast's eye and it howled, staggering back.

"So we're all hunters?" Milla asked.

"I'm an inquisitor who's handled a few," Tubiel said.

"No. I just know the ancient things." Solace loaded another round. "You're the huntress."

"It's real!" Eratta gasped. "Milla, you—"

"I'll take your apology later," she said. "This one, it's unusually tough."

"A dress and jewelry aren't dress for a huntress," Tubiel said. "You can't move like you need to."

"Funnily enough, I was off the job this evening. Solace?"

"It's hiding, but I don't think it's gone." He glanced over at Tubiel. "Nice bracelets, by the way."

The silver bracelets went from his wrist to his elbow. Solace didn't know their significance was, but they were interesting, regardless.

"It was coming for me," Milla said. "How many rounds, Solace?"

"Plenty."

"My mace is buggered." Tubiel held it up.

The ridged head was crumpled.

"I've got enough rounds," Milla said, "but I think this one may be easier to fight during the daytime."

"Agreed," Tubiel said.

Green-Eyes pulled up onto the highest point of the manor and held onto the spire. Its white fur glowed in the moonlight and one of its eyes oozed with blood as it focused on Milla. She stared up at it, while Solace kept aim.

"It's about to attack," Tubiel said. "Solace!"

"I know." Solace fired.

It howled to the sky as blood burst from its other eye, and toppled from the top of the mansion. The breaking of stones echoed as it crashed toward the Grey Hills.

Solace sighed.

"You blinded it," Eratta said. "It won't get far. Let's chase it!"

"No." Solace slung the rifle over his shoulder, by the strap. "I'm going home."

"You have a home?" Tubiel said.

"Funny enough." Solace smiled. "Take care, you three." He drifted back into the forest.

Tomorrow, he'd find Green-Eyes and kill it. Before it killed again.

EXCERPT FROM A HUNTER'S NOTES

Lycanthropes, also called werewolves, were first seen in the southern regions of the Holy Roman Empire. However, at first it was only an affliction of the mind. The sight of the white gleam of the moon triggers something that turns the victim into a raving madman who believes himself a wolf. When wolf attacks would happen, they could trigger someone already suffering from guilt to develop lycanthropy, and thus the understanding that the body would follow came to be.

As a result, the response to the more developed lycanthropes was slow. Why the body eventually follows, or what causes it to follow, whether it be a demon or miasma, is something science can't understand. But it has been discovered that wherever a strange kind of amber—either blue, orange, or green—is found in large quantities, the most unnatural of these beasts will appear.

Lycanthropes can take many forms. It has been reported that some are half-man, half-wolf, and these are the most common kind. All reports indicate that these kinds of werewolves only come into existence by being sired by a high lycanthrope, or body lycanthrope. As a result, wherever a high lycanthrope who doesn't exhibit unnatural abilities appears, it's to be assumed that there's a more powerful one nearby.

It's also to note that there seems to be no pattern as to who can turn into a high lycanthrope. In a case in France, a prisoner who'd been caged through three full moons turned on the fourth full moon and had no access to the means to repress the lycanthropy. In this case, the lycanthrope seemed to be aquatic in nature, adapting to its surroundings of an island prison. It escaped into the water and was later found twenty miles away, with a mind twisted to believe it had never been imprisoned in the first place. Therefore, it's to be assumed that lycanthropes don't know what they are, and their understanding of the world isn't necessarily what's real. This is similar to hysteria—a fundamental departure from reality.

There's a period in which the body hasn't turned, but the mind has. This is a dangerous and incredibly useful time for the beast because it's able to think clearly and move away from the public eye. There's no reason to believe the human side of the lycanthrope has any control over this.
There are a few methods to repress the beast, but this doesn't mean mercy should be given to these individuals who repress it. These people are constantly playing the odds, which is akin to gambling, and therefore are of the devil. The most common is the use of a silver bracelet. It appears that the weak lycanthropes can simply use two loops, whereas the Originators require full braces on their forearms.

It's the gleam of moonlight that turns their mind. Should the sky be covered in dark clouds, or should they lock themselves in complete darkness, they will not turn.
Elderly lycanthropes lose the ability to turn in mind and then in body. As a result, those who have been a lycanthrope for a long time will be

more cunning. Additionally, the beast will grow larger and stronger up until this point. At its apex, an Originator lycanthrope can be immune to their only weakness—silver. To make matters worse, some Originators have proven immune to the last part of the aging process, essentially making them ageless and unkillable on a full moon.

DANIEL

THE MILITIA CAPTAIN

Daniel grunted, trying to steer his horse to face forward. A lazy, rebellious beast and certainly not one of burden. His last horse's leg had crippled when the militia had tried to chase down a thief, and Daniel had to leave it in the forest. So he was stuck on the saddle of this brown-haired horse while leading the militiamen, who joked among themselves about his new horse, and Daniel was torn between anger and laughter, but eventually gave over to laughter.

It had been predicted that there'd be dark skies that night, and it was already cloudy, so the men and women were double-timing the harvest before it became too dark to continue. Miss Shade and Eratta accompanied the militia on their journey through the trees, to the place of the attack, and Daniel was very much jealous of Miss Shade's black stallion. They eventually came to the road.

The Bronzeglade took Daniel's breath away every time. Golden, bronze, and green leaves drifted past them as they trotted through the forest. The trees were a beautiful shade of brown and turned silver at night. Once they came to the bend in the road, Daniel traveled down the narrow path which required them to trot single file. His men began singing, *"His horse is like his lady, he never knows where either one is going!"* and other such lines. Daniel just trotted and smiled, right up until the trees began to give way and they arrived at the gap in the forest caused by a giant stone ridge that ran from one horizon to the other. He turned his horse to travel alongside it, checking that the purple wooden marker was still there. Soon, they could hear the rushing water, and his men stopped singing as they came to the warm pool of white water and a waterfall.

"Sounds like his wife," one of his men muttered.

Daniel laughed and continued trotting his horse to the other side. Once he arrived, he jumped off and tied it up to a nearby tree. His men did the same, while Milla and Eratta remained on horseback, looking confused.

Daniel peered into the water. "We hadn't moved the horse yet, had we?" he asked one of his men.

The man shrugged.

"The horse?" Eratta asked.

"They'd been thrown from the top of the waterfall," Daniel said. "Rider and horse both. The path to and from the monastery is up there."

"And?" Errata said.

"They're both gone," Daniel replied. "The horse died from the fall. The lady broke her leg and crawled up to that rock."

A rock rose from the center of the pool to create a tilted flat surface. There was a flicker of the sun and Daniel looked up to see that someone had come to the edge of the cliff. Solace. His blue ring gleamed in the sunlight.

"Did you see anything?" Daniel called to him.

"Yeah. Too dark to see much, though. There were a few people around here a couple nights ago. Didn't think much of it. Probably some people in the town who're secretly still pagan or something."

"They were covering up a crime," Daniel said. "Did you see anything?"

"No." Solace glanced at Eratta.

Daniel glanced at Eratta, who whispered something to Miss Shade.

"Is there something I should be told?" Daniel asked.

"Come to my estate before dinner," Errata said. "We'll eat and I'll tell you everything. The road up there... I would ask, what was she doing at the monastery?"

"I'll check it out," Daniel said. "Solace, would you be so kind as to help us around?"

"It's big. I don't know everything, but I'll meet you there."

"All right," Daniel said. "And tonight, we talk. Men, say nothing that something could be up. Understood?"

"Yes, sir!" they shouted.

"Let's move!" Daniel jumped back on his horsed and spurred it to a gallop.

The path up to the ridge was a long one, and they rode far past the path that had gotten them to the ridge, down where the rockface had collapsed onto the forest. There, the rocks were small, but Daniel's horse moved quicker than the others, so he got to mock his men as they struggled to make their horses climb. Once they were at the top of the slope, they got to the road on top of the ridge and made the ride for the monastery.

It was a stunning view overlooking the lower part of the Bronzeglade, which included the circle of the town's center and the small houses. While they rode toward the enormous grey hills, Daniel glimpsed the high walls of Eratta's estate through the trees. The road turned back into the forest and the path became more obstructed, but it wasn't long before it became clear and they were in Solace's domain, with runes, visages, and carved epitaphs scattered about.

Finally, they arrived at the monastery, a massive structure, three floors made of white stone. There leftmost side had fallen into a crevice, so an entire side of the building was open, like a shocked mouth. Above the main double doors was a balcony to the second floor, and Solace was sitting on the wall surrounding it.

"The monastery with no origin!" Solace called. "Welcome to one of my humble abodes. I'm not currently staying here at night, but so much to learn."

"All right," Daniel said. "We're going to find out why she came here. Move it, men!"

"Daniel," Solace said, in a sing-song tone. "I've got something here you might be interested to see."

"What?"

Solace smiled. "Staircase is straight ahead."

FATHER BLOSSOM

FATHER BLOSSOM HAD RECEIVED WORD THEY'D RECEIVED A letter two weeks ago. Tubiel had been exiled from the Order two years ago, and the reason why was still unclear. But they answered his call to the town and they would be arriving that morning. Father Blossom had been at odds with the Inquisition before. During his short time away from the town, he saw them in the small port town of Duston, and they burned a witch alive. He didn't know if the man was a witch or warlock, but he knew for sure that killing a man for any reason wasn't the answer.

The militia were off investigating the murder in the woods, and Eratta and Milla had just returned to the estate. So when Father Blossom watched the first horse-drawn carriage come over the hill, he bit his lower lip before muttering a prayer to God and gesturing for the locals to go on their way. The men, women, and children scattered for their home. Mr. Portsman locked the door to the inn, and Mr. Offle closed the door to the brewery. The blacksmith, Mr. Loke, just kept doing his thing, such was the nature of Mr. Loke.

The day was dark and cloudy. Playwrights often wrote about pathetic fallacies—that bad weather heralded dark times—and Father

Blossom was almost able to smile at God's little joke. He made sure his robes were properly fixed. Tubiel, in his regal purple robes, with silver mace and a silver dagger on belt, walked out alongside him and stood in silence. The first carriage came to a stop and the door opened.

"Tubiel, it's been a while!"

A colossal man climbed out. High Inquisitor August. An ancient and strong man with a Scottish accent. He stopped, dusting off his purple robes, and knocked his knuckles against the hilt of his monstrous silver hammer before turning to Father Blossom.

"You must be the local holy man, Father Blossom." August bowed. "Come on, men!"

"Welcome to Bronzeglade," Father Blossom said. "I'm interested as to why Tubiel called you here."

August said nothing and looked at Tubiel, with a grunt, then looked back as the other inquisitors dismounted, in their purple robes. Several in simpler white robes climbed out the back of a wagon and gathered behind the ones with purple robes. All were armed with silver weapons.

"Tubiel is not at liberty to talk about such things," August said. "He is below the whites in our order." He didn't even turn back to face Blossom, but instead counted his men. "But be assured, we come with good reason. Tell me, is the name of the local lord, one Eratta Winters?"

"Yes," Blossom said. "And he will not be happy about having armed men in his town square."

"We'll be on our way soon enough. Once we've solved our little problem. We received the letter two days ago. Has much happened since it was sent, Tubiel?"

"A lot. We're dealing with... *ahem*... an Originator."

August gestured for him to continue.

"Our usual methods did not work."

"So we're dealing with an old beast." August turned to Blossom. "I'll tell you straight. We believe a high lycanthrope lives in your town. A man whose mind became that of a wolf, and his body followed."

"If one of those existed in our town, the bodies would be piled high," Blossom said. "Assuming such beasts exist."

"Oh, they exist," August said. "I've slain eight myself. I used to have a crossbow designed specifically for the job, but it was stolen a week back. Tell me, Father, do you know anything that could assist us?"

"Legends of a green-eyed wolfen that protects this town have existed since the town was built fifty years ago. My predecessor called the Order of Hunters to find it. He believed the myths, but nothing was found. No dead bodies, either. All this was triggered by a death in the forest, which we're not even sure was a murder. And it was probably during the day, because they were riding horseback. I apologize, August. I know of the myths, and they're simply not true. Here in Bronzeglade, anyway. I beg you to leave. I don't want armed men in front of my church!"

"I understand why you're defensive, but we have work to do."

"Do you now?"

Eratta Winters arrived, with a red-haired woman beside him.

"Just the person I wanted to talk to," August said. "I—"

"The green-eyed beast is real," Eratta said. "Miss Shade here is a huntress, and it came for her only two nights ago. We fought it alongside a pagan who lives in the forest, named Solace, and your friend Tubiel. I think if you wish to learn more, Solace knows more than he lets on."

"A pagan?" August said. "The exact kind of person lycanthropy would take—"

"We know he's not a beast," Tubiel said. "Unless he knows some way to stop himself from turning, that we don't."

"And a huntress?" August said. "Usually the men—"

"I'm an only child." Milla spurred her horse forward. "What's your kill count?"

"Eight."

"Seventeen," she hissed. "The one we're dealing with now is far too strong for us to deal with. It's an Originator—incredibly intelligent and unkillable. The best we could do was blind it."

"By—"

"We shot it over two dozen times with silver bullets," Tubiel whispered.

"Don't interrupt me!" August shouted.

"There are two beasts in Bronzeglade," Tubiel said. "Two lycanthropes, both of them Originators."

"Three." August turned to Milla. "Well, Lycan hunting is hardly a woman's job, but if your record is true, then you're smart. What do you say we do?"

"Find out who they are. Keep ourselves secure and safe at night. I've been investigating. He may be a pagan, but you can trust Solace. It's just whether or not he trusts you. And he won't."

"Then I'll—"

"Hurt anyone and my men have orders to kill every one of you," Eratta said. "From all my fief, they'll come and they'll make sure none of you leave alive. Understood?

August stopped smiling, and started to talk again.

"Understand that *you*, August, are nothing more than a vigilante," Errata said. "You are not ordained by her majesty, and I am. I swear by the Danish blood in my veins and the English spirit in my heart that I will ensure you understand your place," He turned his horse's ass to August, and it swished its tail. "And you are not taking the homes of anyone in this town."

"We'll be paying to stay at the White Hart Inn. The white robes will be camping."

Eratta began riding towards his home.

"You underestimate your situation, August." Milla followed Eratta.

"Making a fool of me," August muttered.

"Act a fool," Blossom said, "speak foolish words, boast foolishly.

You are a fool." He turned on his heel, strode home, and slammed the door shut.

He took a few deep breaths. August was going to get people killed, and he wasn't a man of God. He was a man of prideful folly who thought he could hand out God's judgement. And God's judgement is only God's to give.

ATUR

ATUR NOTICED THE PRETTY LADY ON THE HILLSIDE WRITING IN a notebook while sitting on the stone wall which ran along the road on one side of his father's field. She wore black riding leathers that seemed expensive, and her curly hair fell to her shoulders. Artur took a moment to catch his breath. Then he walked over to her.

"Hey, lady!"

She looked up and smiled at him, then returned to writing. Artur rolled his shoulders and sat close to her, on the wall.

She had the grace and decorum of a woman, and every one of her movements was purposeful. She sat with one leg over the other. Her writing was neat, though Artur couldn't read it.

"What's your name?"

"I'm Miss Milla Shade." She didn't look up from her notes. "I'm in town visiting Sir Eratta."

"What's that?" Artur pointed to the thing on her leg.

"That's a pistol. Works like a crossbow."

"Doesn't look like a crossbow."

She shrugged. "It's better than a crossbow." She looked up at him. "What's your name, boy?"

"Artur."

"You should know better than to talk to a lady you haven't been introduced to, or to disrupt someone while they are writing. Remember that."

"But you don't care about that."

Milla's chuckled. "True."

"Where are you from?"

"London. It's a horrible place."

"But it's where the Queen lives!"

"You know, in some places they wear stilts because the filth runs so deep on the streets. And it's full of thieves. There are so many people, you can't just stop somewhere. You always have to keep moving, or they think you're a thief if you're a man, or a whore if you're a woman."

"What's a whore?"

"People don't like women who are whores. But a whore is not for you to speak of or ask of yet. Understood?"

Artur nodded.

"What are you, fifteen?"

"Yeah. I was named last year." He beamed.

"Are you getting married?"

"To a pretty girl." Artur sighed. "Though I don't know who yet. Are you married, Miss Shade?"

"No. I was a nurse over in France until not long ago. I'm seeing if Sir Eratta is worth my time."

"In France? During King Henry's rule?"

"Yes. It's where I learned to keep a pistol with me. It's been a few years since then, I guess. I just haven't found a man worth me."

"But aren't women supposed to marry?"

"And aren't men supposed to be worth my time?"

"Are you worth their time?"

Milla laughed. "Trust me, I'm worth their time."

Artur was silent for a moment. "You're pretty. Lots of men would want to marry you."

"And it makes them forget I'm more than my looks." She put her notebook into her satchel and stepped onto the road. "Take care of yourself, Artur."

"Where are you going?"

"To hunt a wolf." She turned to face him. "I'm a huntress."

Artur laughed. "Men are hunters."

"You know, in the ancient city of Sparta, women were the hunters. I suppose you could say I'm a Spartan."

TUBIEL

THE GOLDEN WOLF

MOST SIGHTINGS OF GREEN-EYES HAD BEEN IN THE Bronzeglade. It had been said that the beast was hard to see because its gleaming white fur blended with the silver trees. The forest stretched across three towns. Bronzeglade was the wealthiest and largest, with a vast marketplace that took an hour to walk. It was also the furthest out, so it much easier to reach.

Gratche was a town was on the other side of the Grey Hills, where the forest stretched along one side. An absurd amount of lumber was produced here, and the wood was coveted for its beauty. But from Tubiel's estimation, Gratche, the third town he'd visited, wasn't the home of the beast. Most of the people who went to that town were labor men from the surrounding towns, and the shadow of the hills meant that the moon wasn't ever-present at night, which greatly reduced the chance of lycanthropy. So Tubiel had resigned to drinking at Gratche's brewery, the Wise Wag. Many gave him odd looks and asked if he was one of the outsiders, because the other purple-robes who'd rolled through that morning wore immaculate purple robes, but his were tattered and dirty. Tubiel told them he was an exile who'd lived in Bronzeglade for years.

He finished his ale and sat back in his seat.

"Are you... are you one of them?" a lady asked.

Tubiel sighed, and when he turned to her, he saw sheer panic on her face.

"Yes." He stood. "What's happened?"

"A giant wolf attacked our house!" she cried.

He looked out of the window. The full moon gleamed through a hole in the grey sky.

"It was big and wreathed in—"

"Fire." He nodded and walked into the center of the brewery. "Any men in here strong enough to wrangle a beast with me!"

"Why?" one of them asked, and then saw the sobbing woman behind him. "Let's go!"

"Take us to your home," Tubiel said to her.

He followed her into the town. Her home was past the lumber mills and was the town's granary, owned by her husband. Except, the granary was now a pile of cinder and rubble, and there was a path of burnt and broken trees leading up to it.

"It took my son and ran off into the forest!"

Why didn't it kill the child? And why would it return?

Solace.

"Does anyone know the way to the old monastery from here?" Tubiel asked.

One of the men shouted that they did and Tubiel gestured for them to lead the way.

"Why?" the woman asked.

"Did you see it take him?" Tubiel said.

"No, but... he fell and the beast chased me, and when I managed to get back, he was gone and couldn't have—"

Wind rushed through the forest. Many men armed themselves with sticks while they trekked. The dark clouds had rolled over the moon, and Tubiel knew they were no longer hunting a beast. The forest finally gave way to open ground and they came out on the other side of the ravine.

Tubiel stared at the side of the monastery and the white bricks that had fallen into the divide.

"Solace, where are you?", Tubiel asked, and he was only answered by silence. "I know you're in here.!"

He said he didn't stay here at night, but this would be where he'd retreat to.

"I'm in here!" Solace called. "But I'm... I'm a bit busy."

"Let the child go, Solace," Tubiel said.

"I saw the burning wolf!" Solace replied. "I saw that this child was hurt!"

Tubiel reached into his robes and pulled out the silver mace. "Find the pagan," he said to the mob. "Do not hurt the child. Do not kill the pagan. Bring them both to me. I know medicine."

The mob rushed to either side of the ravine and stormed the monastery. Tubiel made sure the moon wasn't in the clouds and then joined them.

Like Solace had said, the monastery was colossal. The rooms were furnished, but there seemed to be no rhyme or reason to how it was built. And as they swept through all three floors, it was clear that Solace knew something about this place they didn't. He'd hidden some place, or—

"He's escaped!" Tubiel shouted. "Go out into the forest. Find him!"

The men hurried out of the monastery, shouting.

"Bring them to me. Unharmed!"

Tubiel stayed in the old monastery and sniffed. Now that there was silence, he could smell something. A rich, sweet scent. He followed it back to the divide and peered down into the ravine which the monastery had fallen into. He stood on the edge and wondered if he smelled Solace's medicines. Then he jumped down the rubble and skid to the bottom of the crevice leading into a cave, when his vision was flooded with orange light. He staggered backward and opened his eyes to see a wall of glowing amber, in front of which, Solace was crouched over the injured boy.

"Let him go," Tubiel said.

"You won't stop me. You *can't* stop me."

"Who are you? You're not... you're not entirely human, are you?"

Tubiel looked down at the child, who was laying with his back, with a huge bite wound on his shoulder. Around it, Solace was waving orange smoke. Tubiel gripped his mace and stepped forward, raising his mace. He swore to never abide to witchcraft. Solace was only a pagan, but...

Tubiel stopped once he'd glimpsed past Solace, into the amber, to something within. Solace and the boy were encased in it, elevated. Their black hair went down past their ankles, and their skin was pale. They were dressed in ancient Celtic garb. It was Solace with gleaming green eyes. Tubiel's heart wrenched when the Solace on the outside looked up at him, and he realized he wasn't in a room with just a pagan or a witch. This was worse than any demon.

"I've taken the affliction from him," Solace said. "He won't be a werewolf."

"What are you!"

"I'm a spirit. Diluted to a simple man. I can only channel the powers within this amber."

"Or in that ring." Tubiel gestured the blue one on Solace's finger. "What are you? Some kind of witch alchemist?"

"No." Solace sighed and stood as the orange essence sealed the child's wound shut. "Now to deal with you."

Tubiel stepped forward and Solace's eyes glimmered. Tubiel stopped advancing when he felt his body began to wretch. Solace looked at his forearm as his bracers fractured and began to break. He gasped, staggering back.

"There's no moonlight," Tubiel said. "What... are you the cause of all this?"

"No. I'm here to undo the actions of another who is like me."

"You won't kill me," the Golden Wolf growled. "You won't even let my body turn."

"No, but in this form, your human mind is weak," Solace said.

"So I take from you your memories of this day. You will awake in your bed in the cabin. And in payment for the taking of his memories, I give him a gift."

"What could that be?" the Golden Wolf asked.

"I will separate you both. You will be freed from the human urge to destroy and feed, and you'll be his partner, his golden wolf."

"No, I am my own—"

The orange smoke rushed up the Golden Wolf's nostrils and it staggered back, clutching its throat. It cried out in gasps and fell to its knees. *No, this is mine. I was meant to be the last lycanthrope. I was going to find the cure. I was going to purge—*

Tubiel opened his eyes and yawned. He jumped out of bed, threw on his robes, and opened the door.

"Come on, Golden!" Tubiel patted his leg. "We've got farming to do."

The giant hound looked up to him pulled its body up on its legs, swished its tail, and joined his side.

Tubiel walked out into the bright day and looked out over his view of the forest and the town. Then he checked the irrigation.

THE GREY LADY

"I'M AN OLD LADY IN PAIN, MISS SHADE. HAVEN'T TURNED IN twenty years. Every full moon my mind and body just *try* to turn. I'm a threat to no one. And you would kill my dear Nathaniel's mother? Are you that cruel?"

"I'm a huntress, Miss Flowers," the orange-haired lady said. "I'm simply doing the job I swore to do. I cannot break my oaths."

It was a warm autumn day. The dark clouds had given over to open skies and the sun shone through Miss Flowers's window. News spread fast that the mother of local everyman Nathaniel had turned ill again. The one called Milla Shade had figured it out quickly. Even now, she thumbed over a journal, which Miss Flowers assumed was observations about lycanthropes.

"Awfully pretty dress for a huntress."

"I know." Milla looked up. "What I'm interested in is who sired you. Was it Green-Eyes or Fire-Eyes?"

"Green-Eyes. I have no clue who he is, by the way. He only sired me to save my life. He came in and bit me, gently. That night, I turned. The next day, I was healed."

"So... an act of benevolence?"

51

"Yes"

"Ethelra, may I ask, how come I've never heard of another wolf? A third one."

She showed Milla her bracelets. "Used to stop me from turning. Now they ease the pain."

It was true what Nathaniel had said—Milla Shade was indeed beautiful. But she was like a sour berry. Poisonous killer. The pretty part just made you trust her more. She knew how to dress and paint her face, but the truly beautiful part about her was her hunting instinct. Ethelra knew why this woman was allowed to be a huntress. Because she was extremely adept.

"How long have you been a Lycan?" Milla asked.

"I am not a Lycan. I'm someone with lycanthropy."

Milla remained silent.

"Only... hm, five years. I think I was awfully old to turn. I only turned, what, nine times before it became weaker. The beast is eager. My body, not so much."

"You're being very honest." Milla wrote something.

"You won't find Green-Eyes. He's incredibly smart."

"You were given lycanthropy. Someone who develops it through miasma usually has some kind of strange gift. His must be intelligence."

"He can choose not to turn, you know. I think he has complete control over the beast. Or the beast is human, too."

"How do you know this?"

"Because when I was bitten, I rushed out and saw a man walking away. I didn't see who it was. And you think a Lycan could get inside this house? Preposterous, Miss Shade!"

"He's the toughest lycanthrope I've ever heard of. But I just need to find the man. And you just told me, I'm looking for a man."

"You think in the dark of a night and in the shade of trees I could tell the difference? Goodness, and here I thought you cunning."

"I see why you haven't lied so far. And I survived Green-Eyes once."

"Thanks to the pagan." Ethelra scoffed. "Ugh, to die to you. A serpent. You cannot be trusted, Miss Shade."

"The opposite. I can be trusted. Just don't let me close, if you're a monster."

"Are you sure of that?"

"A woman is dead. An innocent woman. I don't know if it was Green-Eyes or Fire-Eyes, but I know both of them could kill again."

"Green-Eyes is a protector of this town. Its guardian. He wouldn't kill anything if it wasn't a threat to us."

"Then why isn't Fire-Eyes dead?"

"Probably because he doesn't know who it is. It's not easy to identify who's a beast and who isn't."

"That's true."

Ethelra looked down at her withered hands. She was just an old lady in an armchair, at this point.

She smiled. "Have you harmed anyone in the town yet?"

"No."

"Then, are you going to do anything to me? Because that'll make him even angrier. I think after the first time, he decided to back off."

"It was cloudy last night and I've been in safe places every night since then. Not really a chance for him to come for me. And the same will be true tonight. And the next night. Hunt by day, hide by night. It's a simple, reliable process."

"Kill by day, too. You could've at least killed me when it was cloudy. This is too pleasant a day to die."

"This is the perfect day to die. Understand, Ethelra, I don't hate you. I just know that any time an exception is made, something goes terribly wrong. I know that all too well."

"How?"

"What's your preferred way to die?" Milla placed a red apple on Ethelra's lap. "Eat that. It tastes delicious, so I've heard. And it's poisonous, but it's a painless death. Then I'll make your death look like an accident. Like your heart stopped beating in your sleep. You won't suffer, and your son will be able to move on."

"Or you could let me live. But you're too damn stubborn to realize that we're not a danger anymore. That we can control ourselves, and the only time there's a problem is when *someone* comes rolling into town, hunting for us. If you just made us public knowledge, told us how to avoid turning, how to stay safe—"

"You think I haven't heard of that? The problem with lycanthropes isn't the wolf. It's the man. The man avoids admitting what he is. He avoids admitting what will become of him. He makes up some story that the wolf is a gift. That he should share it or let it free. You understand? Man is too foolish with power."

Ethelra looked Milla up and down. "I misjudged you." She picked up the fruit and bit. "You're not a serpent. You're a fox. You hunt, but you won't face the real monster."

"And what would that be?"

Ethelra took a second bite and then set the fruit on the table beside her. "Your fear." She sat back. "Now leave me. I'm going to die like you wanted, and I'll wait for Green-Eyes to send you to me."

Milla wrote one last thing in the journal and then closed it. She put it in her journey and took out a bag of gold.

"I'll leave this under your bed, for Nathaniel to find I do not do this lightly, Miss Flowers. The notebook says to never give lycanthropes a peaceful death."

"Like that makes it better," Ethelra spat.

Milla strode out of her house.

Ethelra sat back and waited for death. A bird landed on the windowsill and tilted its head towards her. The blue bird chirped to the sky and that's where Ethelra went. She didn't go to heaven, but it was still a pleasant place, where all people lived in hues of grey and orange and blue and green. There, she was with her wolf, but the wolf was now mild, stripped of the human desire to glutton, and she found peace.

———

An Excerpt, *The Mind of the Wolf*

...the day I met a lycanthrope who'd been imprisoned in the mountains in the North of Wales. He lived in a cave and had agreed to live there in order for his life to be spared. I found him a surprisingly pleasant man, and I spent a lot of time talking to him. One thing I noticed is that he never realized he was a lycanthrope until he was told of it. He genuinely believed a false narrative of reality, past, present and future. When asked about the bite mark on his arm, he said it was a tattoo he got when he was a sailor going between England and the Pale, and he could describe the history of it in great detail...

UVIRE

THE MILITIAMAN

OFFLE'S WAS THE LARGEST BREWERY IN ERATTA'S FIEF, WITH twelve round tables. Uvire sat at one in the corner, sipping his ale. Funeral preparations for Nathaniel's mother were already underway, and Nathaniel was drinking with him. Losing someone's mother was difficult, but Nathaniel had been expecting it for some time. She'd collapsed in the garden of their home and died looking up at a clear blue sky.

Daniel was with them, too—three old comrades drinking together. They'd hoped Eratta could join them, but he had to oversee the chopping of trees to expand Gratche and to rebuild its granary.

"Lycanthropes." Uvire said. "You really think they exist?"

"Well, do you believe Eratta?" Daniel asked.

"Eratta saw it." Nathaniel said. "It's just hard to believe. Honestly, I'm glad my mother passed while all this was happening, rather than after. If what they're saying is true, this could end in a tragedy."

"We've got to find them," Daniel said. "What do they call them? Green-Eyes and Fire-Eyes?"

"That's it," Tubiel said, from behind Uvire.

"Hey, Tubiel." Nathaniel smiled.

"Care if a join you?"

"Not at all." Nathaniel nodded to an open seat.

"Don't mind Golden." Tubiel gestured to the golden wolfhound beside him. "He's well-behaved."

"I didn't know you had a wolfhound," Uvire said.

"Well, this good behavior is fairly new. I found out he'd had a giant thorn lodged in his paw for about six months." Tubiel sighed, patting the hound. "I feel bad."

"He's beautiful," Nathaniel said. "And massive."

"Keeps my home safe, don't you, boy?" Tubiel beamed.

"You've got a radiance about you that you didn't have when I last saw you," Daniel said. "Did something happen?"

"No." Tubiel shrugged. "Guess I escaped my melancholy. Sorry to hear about your mother, Nathaniel. The natural order can be cruel sometimes."

"Look at this gathering!"

Uvire looked back to see Lady Shade walking towards them. She pulled up a chair and sat beside them, looking down at the golden wolfhound beside her. She rubbed its head and it waggled its pointed ears.

"I'm sorry about your mother, Nathaniel," she said. "Truly. I lost my mother not long ago as well. She was sick, too."

"I was expecting it." He sighed. "She could barely walk and was having these horrible seizures every night. I couldn't imagine the pain she was in."

"She's in a better place now." Lady Shade turned to Uvire. "We haven't properly met, have we?"

"No." He smiled. "I'm Uvire."

"Milla." She nodded. "I heard you were soldiers in France. I was a nurse."

"Nurses. We all relied on them at some point!" Uvire beamed. "I noticed you carry a pistol around with you. Ever used it?"

"Of course. You all know—"

"They know about the Lycans," Tubiel said.

"But they don't know I'm a huntress? Well, what's the point of being a huntress if I can't show off my Spartan spirit?"

Daniel chuckled.

"What's a Spartan?" Nathaniel asked.

"Don't worry about it," Daniel said. "So that's why you're here. The whole thing with Eratta, is that just—"

"No, no," Milla shook her head. "I just caught wind that there was a Lycan when I heard about the murder, right before I got to town. They said it was probably carried out by a giant animal that tossed a horse through the air. I guessed what it was."

"And you two have seen it, right?" Uvire asked.

"Yeah." Tubiel nodded. "Tough motherfucker. Silver bullets usually hurts them, but it was even immune to that. So we have to find the person."

"That's annoying." Uvire sighed. "So much going on in this town at the same time."

"I'm dry." Nathaniel raised his glass.

"Same." Uvire stared down at his empty cup.

"I'll pay for a round." Milla grabbed her pouch and took out three gold coins. "This'll pay for... three rounds, actually. I know you guys are going through a lot at the moment."

"Yeah." Nathaniel smiled. "Thanks."

"No problem." Milla gestured to Mr. Offle. "A round. And two more when I ask for them."

"No problem." He pocketed the coins. "That's enough for four, actually."

Milla chuckled. "Then four it is."

Mr. Offle scooped up the cups and returned to the bar.

"Did any of you know the lady who was murdered?" Milla asked.

"No one even saw her," Daniel said. "And when she was found, she was in full gear for riding. She seemed a city type, like you."

"Huh." Milla looked up in the air. "Interesting. I just want to know what dumb motherfuckers cleared it up."

"Two Lycans," Tubiel said. "They probably walked together. I mean, they could've probably gone back, eaten the horse, and tossed it all down a ravine or something. God knows there's plenty of those in the glade."

Golden began growling, and Milla looked up to see that a man had entered the room. High Inquisitor August, and his inquisitors in their purple and white robes followed him in. The brewery became silent and he pointed to their table. The inquisitors advanced and all five people at the table jumped up. Milla pulled out her pistol and pointed it at the inquisitors.

"You aren't the authority here, August," Milla spat. "What do you want?"

He moved forward, through the mob of inquisitors. "To ask you some questions."

"Then sit and join us like a civilized man," she replied. "You aren't a paleman."

August looked back at his men. "Wait outside."

They turned and marched out. August grabbed a chair and sat between Uvire and Milla.

Uvire glanced out the window. It was getting dark and the blue sky was becoming drenched in orange. Any beasts among them would be revealed now.

"What do you want to know?" Nathaniel asked. "Keep in mind, I'm mourning my mother."

"I know," August said. "But the safety of the townsfolk comes first. Have any of you seen Solace recently?"

Everyone was silent for a moment.

"He came by the market a couple days ago," Nathaniel said. "But I haven't seen anything. Why?"

"I have reason to believe he's a warlock. I think he put the lycanthrope's curse upon this town."

"You really don't know much about Lycans, do you?" Milla said. "It's a disease brought about by miasma."

"Please! A woman isn't educated enough on the essence of

demons and angels. You likely don't even—"

"What are you hoping to achieve?" Milla said.

"Look, while you go around wearing those pretty dresses and fancy jewelry, you don't get to speak down to me."

"You don't get to talk to her like that," Tubiel said.

August turned to him, with his eyes wide and mouth agape. "You—"

"I'm not a part of the Order, remember," Tubiel hissed. "I was too disorderly for you lot of ponces, and—"

"That's not why you were exiled," August said. "And—"

The sky turned red.

"Look," Tubiel said, "you're here because you want to prove that none of us are lycanthropes, right? It's pretty obvious what you need to do."

"Yeah, I'm here to make sure you don't turn." August sighed. "It's the last full moon tonight, anyway. So I guess I have to try this."

"What are you going to do after that?" Milla asked. "If one of us does turn? If one of us is Green-Eyes, you're all fucked. If one of us is Fire-Eyes, this town burns to the ground. Seems like a bad place to confront us."

"Why did you think I wanted to take this outside?" August said.

"Fair." Milla shrugged. "But I don't think any of us are."

"You're all wearing sleeves. Could you lift them? To check you're not—"

A crash resounded, followed by screams. August spun around right as a table was flung across the room and it struck him in the chest. He was thrown over the group's table and the five scrambled to their feet. Others scattered and ran, and Tubiel helped August to his feet.

"It's still dusk." August gasped. "How—"

There it stood, filling the gigantic hole in the wall. Green-Eyes, covered in gleaming white fur. Milla aimed her pistol and fired. The shot hit its eye, knocking its head to the side. Then it turned back to face her. A pistol wasn't powerful enough to penetrate even its eyes.

It pointed at August, eyes full of rage, and then advanced. August scrambled out the door to join his inquisitors. The beast followed.

"Stay away from it!" Tubiel yelled. "It's too strong for us to take on, even with all those inquisitors armed with silver. It'll be a massacre."

Uvire ran to the doorway and saw Green-Eyes in the center of the empty square, the wind whipping its fur. The men in robes surrounded it, all armed with silver weapons—daggers, swords, maces, axes, wood staffs with silver tips. Green-Eyes glanced around.

"Go!" Milla shouted. "Get out of here. Uvire, you too!"

"Are you staying?" Daniel asked her.

"No. I'm just telling you all to get out of here. I know these beasts better than you."

One of the inquisitors swung at Green-Eyes's stomach and his silver sword shattered against the muscle. It swiped the man, with back of its hand and sent him flying through the air, blood spraying from his mouth.

"Now!" August shouted.

The blacksmith's door opened and a giant bolt flew out, struck Green-Eyes in the side, and lodged there. Black blood spurted from the wound. It fell to one knee, howling, and another inquisitor rushed in, axe raised, and swung at its neck. But the head of the axe came off the hilt.

Green-Eyes grabbed the man by the throat. "I am the protector of this town," it growled.

August's eyes bulged and his face became pale, as the inquisitor suffocated in its grasp. It clutched the man's throat tighter and tighter, and blood began to spill from his mouth. Every inquisitor stood in terror as their brother's neck was crushed by this beast's hand.

It took the enormous bolt and pulled it from its flesh. Blue smoke rose from the wound, and it struck another inquisitor across the face. His head flew off, sailing about thirty feet, and splattered against the front of the White Hart Inn.

Green-Eyes stood upright, raising the bolt like a javelin, and aimed straight for August. A howl rolled through the hills in the distance, causing Green-Eyes to pause a split second before he hurled the javelin. The distraction gave August just enough time to leap aside, and the beast bounded down Bronzeglade's main street, towards the source of the howl.

Everyone stood with wide eyes and open mouths, gasping for air. Uvire turned to see that the others had fled as they were told, and he looked back to see that August hadn't dodged the bolt—he'd fainted and was lying in a heap.

Uvire sniffed. Something smelled like the fruit Eratta had once given him. Figs, he remembered they were called.

He shuffled back, turned and sprinted.

ERATTA

THE SUITOR

MISS SHADE LOOKED ESPECIALLY BEAUTIFUL TODAY, IN A flowing blue dress. She'd taken the lift in Eratta's carriage, offered by Mitz, Eratta's black-skinned driver. Milla climbed out of the carriage, smiled at Eratta, and let him take her to his study, where she asked to see his paintings. He was known for being a mad artist, and decided to show Milla the painting he'd done of her. She was on the back of a giant black stallion, in her black riding leathers, her flowing bronze hair the same shade as the leaves floating around her. An image of her arriving in town.

"It's amazing!" Milla beamed. "I'm glad you appreciate the leathers."

"Practical, pretty. They suit you." Eratta held out a finger for each of the three reasons.

She blushed.

"How are you? I heard what happened last night."

"I'm used to that kind of thing. They're not." She sighed. "I think Uvire got shaken up. He saw the whole thing. Said Green-Eyes *spoke*. Which, I should note, is undocumented. Whatever turned him into a high lycanthrope, it must've been a powerful miasma, or... whatever."

"August was looking for Solace," Errata said. "No one's seen him, have they?"

"From what I heard, Tubiel thought he kidnapped a child. My guess is he'll return the child tonight and say he was tending to the child's wounds. Still, he might get scorched for witchcraft."

"Yeah, well, this isn't a safe world for a deist, let alone a pagan."

Deism, Milla thought. *That's—*

"I am a Deist," Errata said. "I see creation, not a creator. That said, I still pray. I'm just waiting on God's light, I suppose."

"Makes sense. Was your father a Christian?"

"He pretended to be, I think. I'm not a lot like my father, you know. He was a proper warrior. Taught me to use a sword and an axe. But I was always better with a rifle. And now, I'm good with neither."

"Looks like you need a strong woman." Milla smiled and nudged him.

"Hopefully I've got one. What do you think of me so far?"

"Well, if this Lycan business goes over smoothly, I think I might stay. As long as you allow me to continue being a huntress, of course."

"Controlling you? Impossible!" Eratta laughed. "And if that's all I'd have to worry about, that'd be fine by me."

"That's fair." Milla giggled.

They strolled into the drawing room, and he fixed two glasses of whiskey. Then they sat in the pair of armchairs. From her seat, on the third floor, Milla could see beyond the walls and out over the Grey Hills. She stared at them with wanderlust.

"Beautiful view, isn't it," Eratta said. "Sounds to me like you've been far and wide."

"I have." Her expression became sullen. "The Shades were a great family of hunters. But a decade ago, all the young men—my cousins and uncles—went on a hunt in South Germany to find a werewolf that was... well, it turned out there was a whole pack of them, and the leader was able to control them. The men of my family fought well, but word of their deaths came to us soon after. Apparently, every beast had been mortally wounded, except the Originator. The alpha. So I took the next boat to Saxony and began my hunt. I went as far as the Ottoman Empire and found them before they could make another town of beasts. I avenged my family and that was my third kill."

"What were the other two?"

"We take part in group hunts of five or six before we're allowed into the world. I probably wasn't ready to face him in Saxony. I'm lucky. I discovered who he was, in a town in Brittany. So when I found him in his human form, he was easy enough to put down."

"That must've been—"

"Hard. Yeah, it was, losing so much of my family. And I loved all of them. Great men. But after that, who was left to carry on the legacy? I was told a woman couldn't, but I pointed to Queen Mary and said, 'But we have a queen.' They would argue that royalty was different, but I don't believe them. Which is why I refuse to marry a man who'll treat me as his property."

"Society—it sucks, doesn't it?" Eratta sighed. "Humans. Sometimes I wonder how much divide there really is between us and wolves. Perhaps, if there is a God, this is his joke to show that people do as much damage as monsters. That we're not so different. We're just as reckless, really."

"Did something happen?"

Eratta sat back in his seat and lowered his head. "Yeah." He gulped his whiskey, then put down his empty glass.

"Tell me."

Eratta poured a second glass and was quiet. Silence hung between them.

Milla put a hand on his shoulder. "You don't have to talk about it if—"

Eratta held up his hand and sighed. "Okay, just... yes. When I was a boy, I grew up in this land. My father had begun turning it into a prosperous town, but at the time people were fearful. They were superstitious, and the legends of the Danish were still strong in their hearts. It was said that demons lived in their hearts and that they fed on human flesh. We convinced most of them, in time, and we thought we were safe.

So I met a girl who'd come from the next fief, and we fell in love. It was young love, but we loved each other. On the day she became a woman and started to bleed, she began suffering from seizures. Her father had a physician see her and the physician said her heart was weak but that she would live. I was committed to her and we loved each other, we really did. And then late one night, a lone man got into the manor. How? I'm still not sure. But the two of us were talking in the gardens, and this man—his name was Tobus—he came with an axe and insisted that the demon inside me had possessed the poor girl. When he advanced on me, she stepped between us. She was so calm and gentle at all times. Opposite of you, really. And she held out her arms and declared, 'He is my love. He is no demon!' And this man cursed us both and put the axe... put it right into her neck. I cried out and a guard found us. The man was executed by hanging three days later, in the largest town square of her father's fief. I still love her, but not in romantic way. I love her in spirit, knowing that while evil people in this world exist, pure people live also."

"What was her name?"

"Teff. Teffly. Funny name, I know. But it suited her."

"She sounds like a good person. Nothing like me."

"I know." Eratta smiled. "You're both beautiful, but in different ways. We'll eat and then you should return to your safe place, wherever it is. We don't want Green-Eyes showing up again."

"He's going after August tonight. It's the last night of the full moon, and I think he knows August is the imminent threat."

"Makes sense." He nodded. "I've got amazing food ready."

"I have to meet your chef. He's so good!"

"He is. Bottoms up, dinner's ready."

"How do you know?"

"I'm the one facing the door." He grinned.

Milla downed the whiskey. "You know, Eratta," she set the glass down, "a warm heart in a man is the most under-celebrated thing in our society. It's funny that your last name is Winters."

TUBIEL'S LOST MEMORY

Tubiel had never been so such a warm place. Even now, as the full moon glistened, it was warm. Spain, the fatherland of inquisitors. All inquisitors followed the teachings from here, and Tubiel was there among the Order of Nox Formadus, the most elite. It was hard to contain his excitement. Fourteen purple-robed inquisitors and three in red robes, honing in on a castle inhabited by werewolves. A difficult mission. The moonlight was useful, but the only path of approach to the island's fort cast a shadow, so it was impossible to see. And they were hunting not just one lycanthrope, but at least four more which had turned at the hand of a second-generation Lycan. Tubiel had proven himself worthy of this expedition by killing the one that sired them, but that wasn't the true test.

He calmed his ego and gripped his mace tighter. The inquisitors stopped advancing, maces ready. A few of them had silver-tipped crossbows, but they were keeping to the rear, with a few white-robes to protect them. A shadow fell over the battlements, and a man stepped out to meet them. The moonlight gleamed off his silver bracelets.

"Inquisitors, welcome," he boomed. "My name is Octavius. I kindly

ask that you leave us be. We wear bracers every night. We are of no risk to you."

"You are a blight," said a red-robe. "You must be purged."

"We will not leave and we will not back down," Octavius said.

"Good. Then we can kill you," the red-robe hissed.

"Very well." Octavius sighed.

Three men and two women stepped up beside him. One more than anticipated. They took off their bracers.

"Fire!" the red-robe shouted.

Crossbows were fired, but they fell wide. The crossbowmen reloaded as the lycanthropes backed away from the edge. First came the cries of the wolves' minds, and then the howls of the Lycan bodies.

Then there was silence.

It was a common phenomenon. The closer to the sire they became, the more influence they had with the other wolves. Octavius had clearly joined the group later, because he seemed the natural leader, and even with Lycan minds, they were like a pack. Staying in the darkness, ready to strike.

Tubiel felt something and smelled something sweet. He looked toward the source of the smell and saw objects had been tossed at the inquisitors, and they had only glanced at it. A piece of blue amber. Tubiel crouched down and picked it up. He turned over its smooth surface and looked deep into it, and something wretched at his heart. He looked up at the terror hanging high in the sky, gleaming white. Beautiful, alluring.

"No," Tubiel gasped, shaking his head. "What..."

The other's ignored him. The battle had begun. The six lycanthropes were crashing in. His body began to shake and twitch. His mind writhed as something unknown began pushing in. Something that had always been there. And without meaning to, Tubiel wailed, and then it seized his mind. He opened his eyes, gasping. His face was against the dirt and blood pooled around his nostrils and lips. A dead lycanthrope lay a few feet away from him, with serrated claw marks on his throat. Tubiel rolled onto his back, sat up, and looked around the scene. It was morning. Bright, warm light dawned on the bloody scene. He looked around and realized there was only one person left standing. The red-robe who'd spoken, except he wasn't standing. He was sitting on a pile of rubble from where part of the castle had collapsed, nursing a wound. He looked up at Tubiel. "You, lycanthrope."

"I don't... it was that blue amber, I swear," Tubiel said.

"I don't care how. You're a lycanthrope. But your mind, not lycanthrope. Your mind was still human."

"I don't remember a thing."

"Hm, no difference. The only things you killed were lycanthropes. That said, you can't be a lycanthrope and an inquisitor. You are exiled from the Order."

"You can't! I earned—"

"You can keep your robes, your texts, your weapons. But you can't keep your rank in the Holy Orders. If you wish to be werewolf hunter, you can be. Otherwise, you can take your vast wealth and become a merchant or gentry man."

"I fought—"

"I thought you dead, but you're not. You showed that God's light blessed you even in your blight. You saved my life. We would've surely lost had you not turned. So I'll take it as a sign from God and decree you disavowed from the Order but let you live and serve as a hunter."

"Fuck you. Fuck the Order."

"Do not insult me. I grant you a mercy. You cannot defeat me. I have God on my side."

"Try me."

The red-robe shook his head. He got to his feet and lifted his sword, but Tubiel realized he was simply cleaning the blood off of it. Red-robe lifted one arm and put his armored gauntlet under the blade, kept his sword pointed forward.

He advanced toward Tubiel. "I was wrong. God didn't save you. Satan did."

"So who won out of those two?" Tubiel looked at the mace in his own hand. "You're full of shit."

"No, I'm—"

Tubiel threw the mace and it smashed into the red-robe's face. He cried out when his nose and cheekbones shattered, and Tubiel rushed forward. The red-robe recovered, blinded by the blood, and swung with his sword in a wide arc. Tubiel ducked below the swipe and pulled his dagger from under his sleeve. He pulled up and plunged the knife into red-robe's throat.

"They'll think I fled after surviving the battle. Fuck you and your Order. You're nothing but scum."

"They'll know." The red-robe gasped. "They'll see the claw wounds on the other lycanthropes and know it was you. You... will die at their hands."

The red-robe died with a smile on his face.

———

A bronze leaf brushed against Tubiel's face as he looked down at the dagger which had been so important to him. It had always served as a reminder, and he didn't know how he could forget something so key. But he had. He couldn't even remember why it had ever been meaningful at all.

Tubiel petted his wolfhound and put the dagger back under his sleeve. The Bronzeglade was strange. The trees whispered among themselves and he could hear them tonight. He could hear the orange that flowed through them, and they were whispering dark omens.

Tubiel stood and peered through the canopy. The full moon was going to remain for one more night, and this time it was blood red. A terrible omen and an even more dreadful gift to the lycanthropes.

He tapped his mace, thinking. The lycanthropes would probably go after their greatest threat—the Inquisition. Tonight, they were at the Winters estate to discuss plans with Eratta. Most of them would be waiting in the gardens. Tubiel wasn't worried about Green-Eyes destroying the Inquisition. He didn't care for them much, anyhow.

No, he was worried for Eratta, because Fire-Eyes was the most destructive lycanthrope Tubiel had ever encountered.

"Come on, boy!" He began jogging.

It was hard to navigate the darkness under the dull red light of the full moon, and Solace burst from the darkness, his cloak flapping about, rifle rattling on his shoulder.

"I see we thought the same thing!" he shouted. "Double time."

Tubiel could see it. He could smell the smoke that wafted through the trees. He bounded from the forest, lost his footing as he vaulted down the slope, and crashed down on the grass. Solace slammed into the wall, shoulder-first, and then they opened the side gate. Tubiel rushed through to see that the inquisitors were in chaos—their usual order and form lost in the throat of battle. In the center of them was an ashen wolf in a deadly brawl. The heat coming from its flesh meant that it was in pain, and every blow that landed caused agonizing burns.

"Stay, boy," Tubiel said to Golden.

The manor was wreathed in flames.

"Has anyone seen Eratta?" Solace shouted.

"He's still in there!" Nathaniel yelled from the other end of the gardens. "I can't... he takes medicines to help him sleep. He won't wake up, not even for this!"

An inquisitor rushed for Fire-Eyes, who turned to meet him. The young man used a long spear to keep his distance. Jab, jab, jab, and the other inquisitors stood ready to attack the moment Fire-Eyes let down its guard. One jab too far and Fire-Eyes slammed a hand on the top of the spear and pinned it to the ground. It looked up at the inquisitor and *smiled*, then leaped and ripped his throat out with its teeth, tossing his lifeless body aside.

Tubiel gasped. "It's intelligent. Like Green-Eyes."

"Yeah, I guessed that much." Solace yanked his rifle off his shoulder. "But not as strong, I can assure you."

An inquisitor's dead body slammed into Solace and trapped him under.

The rifle clattered to the ground and Solace pulled the body off, but it was too late. Fire-Eyes was bounding on all fours, towards them. Tubiel stepped in front and knocked it aside with his mace. The beast crashed against the wall, then rolled back and turned. Solace aimed his rifle and shot it. The round went through its shoulder and it roared. Solace loaded another round and fired again and again. Four shots and it fell to one knee, growling. Solace went to load another round, but it gave one last howl before charging through the wall next to it and into the night. Tubiel looked around at the carnage. Fourteen inquisitors were down and the manor was in flames.

"There's no way in!" Nathaniel hollered. "Eratta! Eratta, wake up!"

The balcony doors above the main doors opened and Eratta stumbled through, disoriented and rushing about. He could feel the fire, hear his home crumbling, but he was still dazed. The pillars began to crack and break, and Solace ran to the steps as the balcony shunted downward. Eratta finally became alert, and while he stared below, his was face struck with terror as the balcony gave way beneath him. Solace was a second too late. Eratta's head crashed against the steps and he began twitching.

"Eratta!" Nathaniel cried.

Solace scooped Eratta in his arms.

"Where are you taking him?" Nathaniel glanced at the inquisitors. They appeared not to care at all about the man who was dying. They weren't even looking.

"I'm taking him to my home, where I can treat his wounds."

"How?" Nathaniel whispered.

"Science you wouldn't understand." Solace rushed off. "No one follow me. That includes you, Tubiel."

———

Uvire sipped his drink. Word was, the pagan had dragged Eratta into the forest. His mother once told him that the souls of men were like

birds—they fly. Uvire looked for birds, but there were none, so he
drank and hoped.

"What're you doing alone, Uvire?" Daniel emerged from the edge of
the crowd.

"You hear about Eratta?" Uvire asked.

"Yeah." Daniel sat across from him.

"You seem fine about it."

"It's Eratta. He'll pull through." Daniel nodded, raising his hand. "A
drink over here! Make a tab."

Uvire narrowed his eyes but hid it behind the bottom of the tankard.

MILLA SHADE

THE HUNTRESS

No one knew what Solace had done, but when he returned Eratta was stable and the twitching had stopped. Solace had said Errata would need about two-weeks rest. Nathaniel transitioned from caring for his mother to taking care of Eratta.

After all the searching, the identity of the two beasts was still unknown. Milla was glad she was facing the window. Nathaniel couldn't see the dark anger that she know was in her eyes.

The nights of full moons was over and the lycanthropes would be able to hide for another month. Then they would come back out. Milla tapped her pistol and realized she was unprepared for what she would be facing. Lycanthropes that could speak were rare, but Green-Eyes and Fire-Eyes weren't the only ones, contrary to what Milla had believed. And after reading some books in Tubiel's library, speaking werewolves only occurred with Originators when there was a large amount of the strange amber present, and even then it wasn't guaranteed.

Regardless, talking beasts couldn't be tracked down by hunting the man. Milla needed to hunt the beast, and she knew exactly how she intended to kill them both. Fire-Eyes would be far easier, but

Green-Eyes wasn't impossible either. She'd planned the murders of both and begun preparing.

She stepped away from the window and took a deep breathe. She'd forgotten that she wasn't a tracker.

"I'm a huntress," she said to herself. "Nathaniel, I'll be leaving town for a few weeks. I'm underprepared for facing the beasts."

"You're going to try!" Nathaniel put a hand to his chest.

"I am. Eratta's a good man. He doesn't deserve this. Doesn't deserve to have a home in pieces. He might not wake up, and quite frankly he's the only man I've met that's slightly worth my time. So I'm going to go get the things I need and then return."

"All right. Take care, Milla."

Milla smiled, but her eyes were sad. "I will." She gave him a hug. "Take care of him, Nathaniel."

"Always."

Milla strode out of the door. She could take the guilt of killing a lycanthrope. It was the people left behind that she couldn't handle.

As she passed through the scorched halls of Eratta's home, down the long staircase, past the craftsmen rebuilding his home, she realized something about Bronzeglade. The people loved their little corner of the world. She walked outside and looked up at the clear blue sky. *Perhaps Green-Eyes is just like them.*

It was common for a huntress to have these doubts, after such a long time on the job. Milla had had left a trail of bodies so far, including The Grey Wolf, an old lady who couldn't even change any more. Milla had put on a strong face, but her heart was turning blue. She needed the month away so that she could ready herself for the most dangerous, most ambitious hunt any hunter had ever attempted.

She wouldn't just find the lycanthrope. She would find the source and end lycanthropy for good. No longer could she believe that the cause was miasma. Her first clue was Tubiel. She'd noticed Tubiel's bracers a while before, and though she was suspicious, she had no proof he was a lycanthrope. Then he emerged a new man, with a giant wolfhound at his side. He'd somehow cured himself of his lycanthropy. Second clue was the blue smoke that came from Green-Eyes's wound. Solace had something that let him carry out medical miracles, and the smoke from Green-Eyes's wound was the same color as Solace's eyes. No one else seemed to have noticed, but what would a huntress be without a sharp eye?

A servant brought Milla her stallion and she climbed on top of it. *Time, preparation, research.* She spurred her horse to a trot and looked back to see Nathaniel standing at the window. She kept riding and the features of his face faded until she could no longer see him anymore. *Perhaps I should've shown mercy. Just once.*

"It's just not the nature of a huntress."

ACT 2

ERATTA

THE CRIPPLED LOVER

Eratta's eyes fluttered open. Today was the day Milla returned to him, and it wasn't the right weather for such an important day.

Apparently, Milla had come to visit him when he was unconscious. It was strange to Eratta that his home had been destroyed and rebuilt and he didn't remember a moment of it. All he knew was that Solace had saved his life. Through what means, he didn't know, but he was long past believing in God and Satan. Perhaps Solace was a practitioner of dark magic, but Eratta knew he wasn't the cause of the lycanthrope curse.

Eratta sat up, pulling his bedsheets to the side, and then flexed the muscles in his arms and legs. They were weak from two weeks of inactivity.

"Good afternoon, Eratta," Milla said, from the corner of the room.

Eratta turned to her. She was sitting in the armchair, holding a glass of whiskey. He jumped out of his bed and ran to her. Wrapped his arms round her and squeezed. She laughed.

"Where'd you go?" he asked.

"I went to prepare." She looked him up and down. "You're naked, by the way."

"Neither of us care." He laughed and started putting on his clothes. "What's your plan, then?"

"I think it's wise to keep that to myself. That said, I will tell you that all my plans are ready. I brought my stuff in the cover of night."

"Your stuff?"

Milla only grinned.

"I see you got a new pistol. Newer?"

"Rare. Much better craftsmanship and can hold more than one bullet at once."

"How?"

"A barrel with eight slots. Fire one and the next slot clicks into place behind the barrel. I have more weapons, and my research has been useful."

"How so?"

"I learned a few things about the nature of the beasts and the possible source of the curse. Do you know of any amber in this town?"

"No, because I would've sold it."

"Huh. Guess you just haven't seen it yet. Eratta, have you noticed Tubiel's wolfhound?"

"Golden?" He nodded. "Yeah."

"I think Tubiel cured his lycanthropy." Milla swirled the glass of whiskey.

Eratta raised an eyebrow. "How could he have done that?"

"He doesn't remember it, I know that. So either the wolf side cured him, or—"

"Solace cured him."

"Solace?"

"He cured me of bleeding inside my head. Cured a child of mortal wounds *and* stopped the onset of lycanthropy. How he does it, I have no idea, but he has a way. I know it."

"Hm. I didn't know about this. Solace lives inside that monastery, right? The one that didn't come from anywhere."

"Yeah." Eratta nodded.

"All right. And you don't think it was witchcraft?"

"He said it was science we didn't understand. And he's a Pagan. He's calling on something, but not the devil."

Milla nodded. "He won't know who the lycanthropes are. He wants to stop them, too, I think. But perhaps he knows the cure. And the cause."

"Perhaps. I'd be careful, though. He's a valuable ally."

"That he is."

"Okay, so what's your plan?"

"Find the cure and kill or cure both lycanthropes."

"Good." Eratta pulled up his coat and checked himself in the long mirror. "You know, there's a fashion now of getting a servant to dress you? It proves that the gentry have lost all self-respect."

"They respect their material goods, including people. What's your plan? It's a full moon in two days."

"Two days..." Eratta sighed. "The Inquisition has informed me that they'll be returning tomorrow. Apparently, August has uncovered some interesting information. I look forward to hearing it."

"He's an amateur." She scoffed and waved a hand in dismissal. "Shall we go down for breakfast?"

Eratta beamed. "I'd like nothing more."

TUBIEL AND GOLDEN

Miss Shade considered herself to be a huntress, but Tubiel thought it was a silly idea, calling someone who hunts monsters a hunter or huntress. A man stalking through the darkness, with his hand cusping the wooden brace of a bow, a finger upon a string, and two more holding the arrow—now that was a hunter. Still, he supposed he was a hunter of Lycans, too.

As he followed the tracks of a deer through the woods, Golden prowled close behind. The moon glistened through the trees, and the trees spoke good omens to Tubiel. This would be a fruitful night, so Tubiel was sure of his path as he trailed through the trees until he could hear rushing water. Then he found himself standing before the White Falls, and there was the deer, feeding from the foam. Tubiel offered a prayer of peace to the animal before releasing the arrow, which whistled and struck home. Golden growled and darted for the deer, then leaped and bit through its throat. It hit the grass with a *thump*, and once again the only sound was the falling water.

Tubiel strolled over to the dead animal and petted Golden. "Good boy." He stopped and sniffed.

A familiar smell, like sour grapes. He followed it up the dark side of the cliff and saw someone standing on the edge, unrecognizable in the darkness. They looked down at Tubiel and held a large white stone up to the moon. Then the stone become its own little moon.

"Forcing a turn?" Tubiel gasped. "But... oh, you son of a bitch!" He turned and sprinted to town.

Golden bounded behind him, through the forest, crashing through the bushes. When Tubiel arrived at his cabin, set down his bow and quiver and grabbed his mace and dagger before continuing toward the town. As he descended the hill, he saw that a dark cloud had engulfed the sky, and he was soon running through lashing silver rain. It ran down his face and soaked his robes, but he continued, his feet splashing through potholes and cobbles. He darted his gaze around, trying to see Green-Eyes, but he couldn't. He encountered an empty market square and crept through it, listening, but couldn't hear anything. He tiptoed to the White Hart Inn and silently opened the front door.

"Tubiel?" Mr. Portsman said. "Sorry, not serving—"

Tubiel put his finger to his lips and moved to the staircase. Mr. Portsman escaped to the back room. As Tubiel ascended the stairs, it was completely silent throughout the inn. He could only hear his footsteps and the rain against the tall windows overlooking the staircase and the wooden walls. One by one, he stepped, slow and creaking.

He finally got to Milla's room at the top, the best room in the inn, and slowly opened the door. It creaked and Milla dived out of bed. She threw her hand under her pillow and came up with a strange pistol pointed at him.

"What are you doing here, Tubiel?"

Thunder shocked the room and shattering glass cut through the air as Green-Eyes flew through the window. He skidded across the wet floor and banged against the wall. Milla took aim, but Tubiel stepped between them and sprayed mace on the wolf's face, shoulder, and across the face again. Then a single swipe hurled him across the room and left him in a crumpled heap. He looked up at Milla as

Green-Eyes rushed toward her. She fired, and fired, and fired, and fired, and fired, and fired, and fired, and fired again. Green-Eyes staggered back. Eight rounds in one gun, and these hit harder. One of its eyes seeped black blood and he lashed at Milla. She ducked his blow and slid across the floor, where she pulled something out from under her bed and fired it at Green-Eyes. The beast flew backward, slammed through the wall, and went tumbling down the staircase in a spray of black blood.

The sound of this new gun made Tubiel's ears howl.

"What was that?" He fell to his knees. His stomach and ribs hurt like hell.

"A blunderbuss." Milla reloaded for another shot. "Sorry, I've only got one."

Tubiel got to his feet, clutching his mace. "Where did that fucker go?"

"He's quiet and smart. He won't do anything to risk anyone else's life." She turned to Tubiel. "It isn't a full moon, is it?"

"I saw him use some sort of stone to focus the moonlight but couldn't make out who it was. I was hunting by starlight."

"Son of a bitch. Wasn't expecting to have to fight him here. I don't have the means."

"Then we don't fight him here. We find a way out."

The thatching and wooden rafters broke open, and Green-Eyes grabbed Tubiel's arm. He spun, bashing its elbow with his mace, but it lifted him up into the night's sky, where all Tubiel could see was stars and gleaming green eyes. It studied him, tilting its head. Tubiel swung again and it snatched the mace out of his hands and tossed it into the market square below.

"How?" the beast asked.

Tubiel slung the dagger out of his sleeve and plunged it into Green-Eyes's wounded eye. It roared, thrashing about, and tossed Tubiel onto the blacksmith's stone rooftop, where his forearm crunched against the surface. Green-Eyes was then hit again by the blunderbuss, and was catapulted off the rooftop, down to the market square, where the cobbles cracked beneath his weight. Green-Eyes lay still.

"Did she—"

As the beast rolled onto his front and climbed to his feet, Golden charged in and leaped toward it. Green-Eyes turned to the wolfhound, with wide eyes, then howled when Golden latched onto its arm and sunk its teeth in, drawing black blood. Green-Eyes threw Golden off and he landed on his feet. The great white retreated down the street as the townsfolk peered from the shadows.

Tubiel hissed, dragging himself to the edge of the rooftop. "Anyone mind..." He gasped, with a chuckle, "giving me a hand? Mine isn't working."

"Tubiel!" Milla climbed through the hole in the rooftop. "Where—"

"Green-Eyes left. I stabbed him in the eye. Think I nearly killed him." He gasped again. "Milla, my arm is fucked."

"What happened?" someone shouted. "Have the demon wolves returned?"

"Yup!" Tubiel called back. "Now can someone please get me off this rooftop."

BLOSSOM

THE PRIEST

ANOTHER CHAOTIC NIGHT AND COLD MORNING. HARVEST season was reaching its end, and the wind was frigid. It also rained every other night. Father Blossom returned from the forest with his basket of freshly picked flowers and herbs.

There was a crater in the middle of the town square and the militia were running about. They'd asked Blossom if he'd seen Green-Eyes, to which he answered no. Everything was going to shit. He could tell the war between man and lycanthrope was about to reach a breaking point. Could feel the devil weaving his trap upon the hearts of the people as they became eager to kill. Tomorrow night, what might happen? Green-Eyes may kill someone. Fire-Eyes could burn down a village. Perhaps one of them would die, and that still wouldn't be good. Only peace was needed.

It was sunrise and it had stopped raining. Apparently, it had been a nightmare getting Tubiel down, but Milla had seen to his injuries well enough. Still, from what Blossom had heard, Tubiel was the only person hunting the Lycanthropes who wasn't dogmatic about it. And with him now being unable to fight, it now seemed that the war would not only be savage, but reckless. The collateral damage could be terrible, and several people would die.

"Father!" Milla called, leaving the White Hart Inn. "I haven't seen you yet."

"I was out getting herbs, as usual. Did the green-eyed one try and get you through the roof?"

"He came through the window first. Thankfully, Tubiel saw him first. Said he had some kind of... moonstone, and then he turned."

"Does that mean he knows what he is?"

Milla chuckled. "No."

"Damn." Blossom sighed. "I was hoping we could imprison—"

"No prisons. This is the most dangerous lycanthrope I've ever seen. He's intelligent, cunning, and murderous."

"Why is he hunting you? Why go through the effort of using a... did you call it a moonstone?"

"Don't think it was effort. And why? I've got two dozen lycanthrope kills under my belt. I'm dangerous and I just proved it to him."

"You really must be dangerous. You survived. It's funny, I've yet to see either of them. I would think, though, that the priority is Fire-Eyes."

"Yes, unfortunately they're more than illusive. Where and when Fire-Eyes strikes seems to be random. No pattern, other than carnage. We know Green-Eyes is a protector, so I can predict his behavior. But Fire-Eyes, I'll just have to hunt down the old-fashioned way."

"You better be well-prepared. I don't want the townspeople getting hurt. Do it *far* from this town, or I'll see to it that your nobility means nothing, Miss Shade. Do you understand?"

"Don't worry about that."

"And I don't want you in the town, either. So do your work and leave."

She scoffed and frowned. "Why are you suddenly so offended?"

He sighed. "Because you killed someone who wasn't a danger, out of sheer dogmatism."

Milla was silent and guilt flashed in her eyes.

Blossom's heart sank.

"Do you know what happens in the late stages?" she asked. "The beast, it fights. And it'll push the body beyond its limit. It'll kill the human by pushing the bones out of the flesh, creating the most agonizing death possible. And the seizures are just the start of it. The body stops being able to return to normal, and she would've died slowly, painfully as her body deformed."

He shrugged off his anger. "Fine. Was it painless?"

"Of course."

"Still doesn't excuse it." He sighed. "I'll pray for you, Miss Shade."

"Will you?" She stormed off.

Blossom looked at the sky. "Lord, sometimes you make my task difficult. And I think you're lying to me."

AVEM

Avem Advent always relished in the small-town feel of Bronzeglade, and the place reminded her of her sister, because that's where she went to visit Eratta. She fell in love there and died there. Her father, who was lord of the next fief next door, had held a funeral for her in Bronzeglade. She was a girl of two places.

Avem's favorite spot was a place that very few new about—an old Celtic druid's ground. The stones and the oaks were still scored with their markings. A magnificent place where the bronze leaves swirled in the wind.

"This is where we would play, wasn't it, Avem?" Eratta laughed. "It's been too long."

Avem smiled. Eratta's arm was linked with Miss Shade, a stunning woman who seemed comfortable with him. And he was just as comfortable with her. Avem smiled at them and sat on one of the stones.

"Milla, this is Avem, Teffly's sister. Avem, this is Milla."

"Heard you two are getting married," Avem said. "As Teffly's sister, it's my job to rip your head off if you hurt him."

"I wouldn't," Milla said. "Though..."

"What?" Avem asked.

"What do you know about the happenings recently?"

Eratta raised his hand to protest.

Avem shrugged. "Heard you have monstrous wolves running about the place, causing all kinds of chaos."

"Fair enough. Just curious."

"This was where Teffly and I met," Errata said to Milla. "The two sisters—identical twins, actually—would come here to play. Their father is... well, he was a carefree fellow, and lets his daughters wander the woods. No boars or anything, and there'd always be a crew of servants and guards a shout away, so they'd play here. Anyway, I was being taught to hunt by my father's huntsman, Paul, and I decided to get lost and meet up with the sisters. Avem didn't like me much."

"I didn't like you for a long time," she said.

"You liked me eventually." Eratta smiled. "Anyway, Avem said she didn't trust me because my father was Danish. You know about that. But Teffly gave me a hug and told Avem to shut up."

"It's true." Avem beamed. "And I did eventually become fond of Eratta. He made my sister happy. I'm amazed you haven't been married off, Milla."

"I was a nurse in France for a while."

"Not a future lady's job." Avem frowned.

"I wanted to explore the world. Pretended to be a common girl, which almost got me killed."

"What happened?" Avem asked.

"The camp was attacked and I killed the three soldiers that found me."

"Pretending to be a common girl—why?"

"Because the gentry always bored me. Still do, mostly. I was going to be married off, which I just couldn't stand for."

"It was your duty."

"It's my duty to continue my family's name, and I wasn't going to marry some pathetic man with no strength of heart. I'm the only remaining member of the Shade family who can have children."

"Wha—"

"Eratta, she's upsetting me." Milla turned to face him. "I don't like her... outlook."

"Milla, she's a friend."

She glared at Avem.

"She's like Teffly," Avem said to Eratta.

"They both speak their minds and they both love nature, that's true." He chuckled. "But Milla's quite different."

"She's not as—"

"Teffly would be angry because you were mean to me. Milla's angry because she thinks you were rude to her. But both of you are good people with very different outlooks. You'd have a lot in common, though."

Neither woman said anything.

Eratta sighed. "Are you going to be spending a few days? You've got to know that now is a bad time, with those giant wolves are still about. I nearly died."

"But I'd be—"

"I can't tell you exactly what's going on," Eratta said. "But right now, being in this town is dangerous. Only last night, there was an attack at the White Hart. One man broke his—"

"Then why is she here?" Avem glared at Milla. "Why are you here?"

Milla didn't say anything. Eratta also remained silent, his long white hair draping around his face, and he could see Avem out of the corner of his eye. She looked at him and them back to Milla, who was dressed in black riding leathers, with a strange gun strapped to her leg. She started back at Avem, with her deep blue eyes.

"Is there... wait, there are actually lycanthropes? And you, Milla, you're really a huntress?"

"Last of a long line." She grinned. "I plan on ending lycanthropy once and for all."

"Like a spartan," Avem said.

"I said that myself, only a month ago." Milla laughed. "Look, I'm skilled. I have piles of lycanthrope bodies behind me. I'm armed with weaponry that you *cannot* get, decades ahead of its time. And even then, I nearly died."

"Did it attack you?"

"Twice. The white-furred one."

"Huh... why?"

"I'm a huntress, so I'm a threat."

"Makes sense." Avem nodded.

"Avem, can I ask you something?" Eratta said.

"Yes."

"You asked if it attacked her, but it's well-known that there are two lycanthropes."

Avem shrugged. "Sorry, I'm not staying up to date."

"Show us your wrists," Milla said.

"Why?"

"Just do it, Avem."

Avem showed Milla her naked wrists.

"Okay." Milla sighed. "Want to join us for dinner tonight?"

"Sure. "The Winters manor, I assume?"

"I'll allow it." Eratta chortled.

Avem peered around the druid's circle. She could hear a faint noise, so she focused in. The trees were whispering to each other. They spoke of a power somewhere deep within the earth, and from it all things flowed. Some of the power had escaped to the surface, and this fragment tried to seal the rest underground. Eratta was speaking to Milla, but Avem could only hear the rustling trees and the silence of the stones. This piece of power took the form of a mortal man so that it could be conducted more efficiently. The trees spoke of a ritual that fused this world with another. The moon and how this world was now beset by it.

Avem looked up and saw a night's sky with no stars. Only the bright moon covering the sky and getting closer, bearing down upon the world. She could feel its power seeping through her veins, and tried to pull herself free. She fell to the ground and felt Eratta and Milla yelling at her. Now she stood in the center of the druid's circle.

There was something lurking in the shadow of the trees. It was in the likeness of a man, but its head was that of a skinned deer and two bloody antlers rose from his head. Avem just stared at him. His hands were like bear paws and his teeth were fanged.

"Get out!" it yelled.

Avem's eyes fluttered open.

SOLACE BLUE

Solace felt it. The pulse of energy rushing through the trees which spoke to each other. The ancient art of Druidry was one that came naturally to some people. Harnessed, it was a great thing. When you entered the world of the spirits and walked among them, as Solace did now, you could hear all of them communicating with each other. A level of existence that not even the God of this world could reach.

The trees spoke of another who'd arrived in this world but didn't know where they were. And as quick as the panicked whispers had begun, they stopped on command from a spirit of great power, and the new druid was gone.

Solace flighted himself to the druid's circle, where he peered into the world of mortals. Avem, with Milla and Eratta helping her to her feet.

"What are you doing here, Solace Blue?" Wreath asked.

"I came to see. Did you command them to leave?"

"Yes."

"Foolish."

Wreath's head turned red with anger. Solace glared at him and

Wreath settled himself. Solace looked to the sky and saw the spirit of the moon, so close to this place where the worlds fused. He cast himself from the world of the spirits and opened his eyes. Got up and stretched, then looked back at the giant wall of glowing amber.

"What are you?" Tubiel asked, from the edge of the cave.

Solace beckoned him and Tubiel came to his side. Solace pointed to the amber.

"I was wondering about that," Tubiel said. "Are you... his soul?"

"Close. You see, what lies in there is the most powerful of all the spirits—a being called Solace. His soul was fractured into a thousand pieces and he has scoured the world to find those pieces."

"What are those pieces?"

"Orange. There's a spirit called Makh. He's one of humanity's many guardians. The most human of all spirits. He saw how powerful Solace was, so he transformed some of that power into amber blue." Solace held up the silver ring and the blue amber that gleamed within. "Solace was drawn to the amber. It was his soul, after all. So he broke open Heron's Mound, descended into the depths and took the ring. So blinded by his victory, at long last, he hurried back and returned to his hiding place in this cave. What he didn't realize was that I could no longer be a part of him. So I broke myself apart and made his soul burst from his chest. It came out in the form of orange amber."

"So you're..."

"I'm Solace Blue. I have no power. The only way I can access power is to steal it from him. But he can't move."

"But his power is free. It has its own mind."

"Something else happened in this town many years ago. This world partially fused with the world of the spirits and the essence of the moon spirit fused with this amber. As a result, this town has produced nine powerful lycanthropes in sixty years. Only two, maybe three remain in Bronzeglade." Solace slapped his hand on the amber. "And I don't know who either of them are. Can't trace them. Can't... sense them. The spirit of the moon doesn't talk and it's too far away to be spoken to. So I just have to try and undo the stupid mistakes of what *was* me."

"I've seen what you can do." Tubiel took a step closer. "Solace, was I... did you take away my lycanthropy?" He glanced over at Golden.

"Yes."

"Thank you." Tubiel smiled.

Solace smiled back. "I live inside this ring." He held it up. "The Solace you knew before, was the one who was looking for the pieces of his soul."

"Don't you desire them?"

"No. My hope is to get the lycanthropes down here, and if everything has gone as planned, Green-Eyes will be coming to me tonight."

"Can you defeat him?"

"Possibly not, but I'll try. Will you help me?"

"Of course." Tubiel nodded.

"Good. Now, we wait."

ERATTA

Shortly after Avem fainted, the snow began to fall heavy. Eratta sat inside, and ordered for the fireplaces to be ignited. He sent out laborers to collect extra firewood, and waited. But as the snow began to grow thicker and thicker, the Inquisition had yet to arrive yet.

Eratta pouted his lips and sighed. Milla was sitting by the fireplace, reading a book titled *The Curiosity of Amber and its Applications in the Unnatural Arts*, and taking notes in her notebook. Eratta took one last look over his lodge book and signed his letter confirming his plans for the winter. Then he heard a chirp and looked toward the window, where a bird was perched on the windowsill. It turned its head twice before taking flight into the snowy sky.

"I'm getting worried," Eratta said. "The Inquisition should be here by now."

"Perhaps they're doing something they don't want you to know about," Milla said.

"It's possible. And the snow is falling thick and fast. They'll have free reign, if they're crazy enough."

"They are. What are you going to do about it?"

"Call the militia. But...

"What?"

"I don't trust Daniel."

Milla turned to Eratta, frowning. "Why?"

"Well... the night I was taken by Solace, Nathaniel sent a servant to the militia, but Daniel was never at home. His wife was too sick to know what could've possibly been happening and he refuses to tell me where he was."

"Nathaniel told you this?"

"Yes."

"Where's Nathaniel?"

"I don't know. Once he was done taking care of me... I think the man needs a rest. He's been through too much for one man."

"Hm. Don't let the man hide the beast. The beast hides from the man, and a pure heart is the most blind. There are lots of pure hearts in this town, Eratta. You included."

"My suspicions are fair."

"True." Milla nodded. "Sorry, my mind... there's a lot of strange stuff being talked about here." She looked down at her book. "It says there's three kinds of amber... orange, blue, and green. Orange amber is the source of unnatural gifts."

"I see it in my dreams."

Milla narrowed her eyes at him. "Why?" She paused. "Solace. That's how Solace healed you! And blue is for unnatural spirits. Made spirits or non-human souls."

"Who wrote this?"

"I don't know." She flicked through the pages. "I see. They used the name Apophis. The Egyptians thought he was a god, I believe. He was probably just a practitioner of witchcraft."

"And Solace is a... witch? He must have a lot of that amber."

"I'm not a witch hunter. And I like Solace, so I won't hunt him or even expose him. But it looks that way." She looked up at the ceiling. "Apophis writes that there are many human witches, and there are many spirits that take a human form. And I've been wondering some-thing about Solace."

"What?"

"He lives out there, right? In the woods? The only things he comes in town to buy are pies and pastries. Never bread or vegeta-bles. Like he only eats for pleasure. And he can flit around the hills faster than people can on flat ground. He never sleeps. He's... I think he's a spirit."

"Well, what can we learn from that?"

"I don't know." She shook her head. "I don't know."

"Actually, it teaches us one thing. That Solace, and I'm guessing the monastery too, isn't going to tell us how to deal with the pair of wolves in town. We need to do this the old-fashioned way."

Milla thought for a moment. "Tubiel... did you notice how he suddenly turned up with a wolfhound?"

"Yeah."

"I think Solace cured his lycanthropy. I think Solace can reverse it. He could heal you and that child."

"I wouldn't risk Solace *healing* them." Eratta shook his head.

"I agree. But that's probably what he's planning to do. Which is why he tried to blind Green-Eyes rather than kill him."

Eratta sighed and sat back in his seat. Looked out of the window again. The guards had taken a short break to wrap up in furs, and were now back in position on the walls. Eratta looked over the gardens. The flowers would be dead by evening. The trees were already beginning to strip bare, though they'd lasted longer than most. A Northern wind had come, reminding Eratta of the bad omens his father used to always speak about.

He got up and roamed to the back door, leaving Milla by the fire-place, and opened the doors. The frigid wind rattled his bones. He took a deep breath and stepped out into the now-trickling snow. The skies parted and the door slammed shut behind him.

"Eratta Winters!" someone shouted

He turned around to an inquisitor with one hand on the doorknob and the other holding a long silver blade. Eratta stepped back, but his weakened legs couldn't handle the sudden movement and he crashed down into the snow. A second inquisitor was standing by a nearby bush. After looking through the window, into the room Milla was in, he nodded to the first, then slid from behind the shrub and began to approach. Eratta looked around and saw six hiding around the place. The guard on the wall had his rifle aimed at Eratta.

"Milla! Help!" he shouted, then jumped up and drew his sword.

A gunshot blasted and the guard atop the wall toppled down onto the snow. The inquisitors turned to Milla as she stepped out of the huge window of Eratta's study and into the snow. She loaded another bullet into the revolver.

"Eratta, you stand accused of being a lycanthrope," one of the inquisitors said. "How do you plead?"

"I am no lycanthrope," he hissed. "I'm a goddamn Dane."

"Denial? Then there can be no expulsion of the demon before you die."

The first attacked with a silver axe. But Eratta, a trained swordsman with the skill of an Englishman and the might of a Dane, parried and sliced and the inquisitor staggered backward, clutching his throat, with blood spilling from it. He toppled to the snow, and the birds perched upon the trees took flight.

More inquisitors attacked. Milla fired six times and their heads cracked open like eggs. Their bodies toppled to the snow in bloody heaps, with a crunch. Milla looked down to reload just as another one of Errata's guards step out onto the wall, wielding a crossbow. She snapped the revolver shut and the guard shot at Milla, but Eratta in front of her. The arrow went through his stomach and lodged in his back. He gasped and staggered back. Another gunshot echoed and the guard toppled out of view. Eratta hit the snow, gasping, looking at an open blue sky. The snow was icy and comforting against his cheeks. Milla fell to her knees, beside him.

"Eratta! No, no, no. Why... why did they think... were you..."

"Of course not." He sighed. "But it's just like what happened to Teffly, isn't it? Fear and ignorance, always."

"You're badly wounded. I can... I don't... no, my—"

"I'm about... to lose strength. Milla, you're the most beautiful thing in this world, in soul and body. Just make sure your mind... finds peace, too."

Eratta went on to the place of his fathers and waited for Milla to come to him. He smiled all the way.

DANIEL

Errata lay on his back, with a content expression, surrounded by six dead inquisitors. Uvire called out that he'd found a guard dead on the wall. All of them had suffered from gunshot wounds, except one who'd been sliced up by Eratta's blade. The snow had melted into a thick pool of water filled with red.

Daniel looked around. "Has anyone seen Miss Shade?" he shouted.

His men shook their heads.

Daniel crouched down and studied the dead men. All six had headshots, and he remembered seeing Milla's new gun, which could hold eight bullets. She must've shot the two guards as well.

"Miss Shade has gone to take revenge for this!" Daniel said. "Does anyone know the current whereabouts of High Inquisitor August?"

"Redrock!" Uvire called back.

"Good job," Daniel said. "Did anyone see anything?"

"I just got done with a witness," one of his men said, from the door. "They said they came out to see Miss Shade surrounded by dead bodies. She was holding Eratta in her arms. Then she got on her stallion and rode out of the estate."

"We will find August," Daniel said. "All this is to be considered self-defense on the part of Milla. August is in charge of these inquisitors and he will be prosecuted as such. Mount up!"

As his men hurried to the front of the estate, Daniel took one last look at Eratta laying in the cold.

"I would stop to mourn," he sighed and smiled, "but I know you'd want me to make sure Milla's safe. So to Milla I'll go."

He sprinted ran to the front gate, where his fourteen men had already mounted their horses, with new silver-bullet rifles on their shoulders. Daniel spurred his horse to gallop and his men followed. Redrock was a town that mined silver, in the hills, and they rode to the base of the mountain, through trails of trees, open roads, and narrow paths. Finally, they broke from the trees to the plain of the long-grassed hillside, and Daniel pulled his horse to a stop.

There laid a white-robed inquisitor on their back, with blood pouring from two gunshot wounds in the chest. A silver-tipped staff lay on the grass beside him. Daniel trailed the horse up to where a purple-robe and another white-robe lay. One of them had no head, and the other had bled out after leaving a smear of blood during the crawl to try to reach safety.

"A lady did this?" one of the men asked.

"Miss Shade is barely human," Daniel said.

They continued up the hillside, towards the town. The sun stood at the top of the hill and beamed between the large stone houses. There Milla stood, outlined in the shadows, surrounded by empty streets and quiet buildings. She glanced back at Daniel and marched deeper into the town.

"Milla!" He spurred his horse into a gallop up the hill and onto the streets, then halted.

Milla was standing in the town square, and doors all around were opening as the inquisitors spilled out. She took fire and the carnage began. The inquisitors tried to attack, but Milla was faster than any mortal being Daniel had seen. With the fire of pain in her heart, she shot accurately and reloaded quickly, and the men fell as fast as they came. They started trying to climb over one another, but Milla kept shooting. Daniel held his hands up, knowing she might reflexively shoot anyone who approached. Eventually, she stood alone, the last inquisitor barely only crawling a foot away from her before toppling over.

She tossed his limp body aside and shrieked, "August, you sick bastard! Face me like a man!"

"High Inquisitor August, by the power vested in me by my lord," Daniel trailed his horse into the town square, "and following the wishes of my Lord Eratta for me to serve Miss Shade should he die during the events of this town, you are under arrest for the murder of Lord Eratta. Come into the light and face God's judgment."

The doors to the town hall opened, and August walked out, shrouded in a rich red robe, holding a two-handed war hammer in both hands. He was armored in head-to-toe in silver and he pointed his weapon at Milla.

"Fire!" Daniel commanded.

His men fired in a volley, but the bullets bounces off August's armor.

"I've got him," Milla hissed.

"He's fully armored," Daniel said. "In resisting arrest, High Inquisitor August, your life is forfeit. Anyone who kills you will not be charged with any crime."

"You are of the devil, Daniel and Milla," August said. "And I'll kill you both."

Milla advanced, her navy dressed billowing. August moved towards her and threw up his hammer. She fired a shot and August cried out. The shot had gone through the plating on his wrist and he staggered back. He tried to wield the hammer with one hand, but a shot to the shoulder rendered his arm useless. He cursed, reaching for a blade, and Milla kicked him in the jaw, which launched him onto his back.

"The first man I've loved in a long time, and you killed him! You are not a man of God. I hope you enjoy damnation."

August lay on his back, with wide eyes. It appeared he was realizing that all his righteousness was nothing more than arrogance.

Milla was deadlier than the greatest warrior, because she was a huntress. August had been her prey, and she'd left dead bodies piled all around the town square on her path to get to him.

"Fuck you." She snatched off his breast piece to reveal bare chest. Pressed the silver gun against his heart and fired.

The shot resounded through town, captured by the curious eyes, and August became still. Milla stepped away from his body and strode away. Daniel began to ride towards her, but stopped.

Now that she'd hunted, she needed to rest.

SOLACE

Solace opened his eyes. The trees' warning whispers became silent as he took in his surroundings. He listened to the spirits and they answered. While standing at the steps of the monastery, he saw it. It raked its claws through the bark of the trees, and the beast's eyes flashed green in the darkness. It rose, towering three times the height of a man, with a vicious grin. Its eyes gleamed white and it stepped from the trees.

"You reek," Green-Eyes growled.

A tree toppled over and crashed behind it.

"You're not human," it said.

"No, I'm a spirit," Solace said

It looked around and saw Tubiel leaning against a tree, with mace on his hip and a wolfhound at his side.

"He reeks, too," the beast roared. "He was a Lycan."

"Correct." Solace nodded. "And I cured him. I offer the same thing to you."

It shook its head.

Solace nodded. "I wish to see the lycanthrope threat ended, by any means. I'll force the wolf and the man within you apart, as I did with Tubiel."

"It's this union that allows me to protect," it growled.

"I just want to know who Fire-Eyes is," Solace said.

Green-Eyes began to speak, but snapped its teeth and choked and thrashed its head about. Then it righted itself.

"Seems it can't betray one of its pack," Tubiel said.

The sky was clear, and Solace listened to the trees as they whispered dark omens. They spoke of death coming soon. Of a tragedy, and Solace asked them who this tragedy would fall upon, but they didn't know.

Green-Eyes stared at both of them.

"Do you have worshippers in the town?" Solace asked Green-Eyes.

"Yes," it replied.

"Who?"

It didn't respond.

The wind howled.

"Now!" Solace shouted.

From the shadows, Nathaniel hurled a spear and it sliced through Green-Eyes's arm. Tubiel rushed toward it, silver-laced rope in hand, and grabbed Green-Eyes's other arm. The beast thrashed and threw Tubiel through the air. He crashed to the dirt. It ripped the spear from its flesh and sliced his claws through the rope, then howled right as the ground began to glow with orange light. Solace hurled the amber at Green-Eyes, locked it around his chest and shunted him into the ground. The beast hit the dirt, and Solace felt the heat of the glow, which rose in orange smoke. With invisible strings, he forced Green-Eyes up onto its knees, then poured the smoke through his maw and nose, and the tether was made. He reached deep to find the man so that he could set him free. But he found that a wolf and a man weren't trapped together. It was a whole blue spirit.

Green-Eyes tore itself free. Solace pulled his mind back to the mortal realm right as Green-Eyes charged into him and slashed its claw through his stomach.

"Solace!" Tubiel and Nathaniel shouted.

His guts splattered on the dirt and he fell to one knee.

"Fuck!" Solace gasped.

Green-Eyes reared up and charged off into the darkness.

Tubiel kneeled beside him. "Solace, can you—"

"No, I can't heal myself." He sighed.

"Aren't you... Solace, you're dying."

"I suppose so."

"Aren't you—"

"I'm not even meant to be alive, Nathaniel."

"He doesn't even know which of us is talking," Tubiel said.

"He's dying, Tubiel," Nathaniel said.

"No, no, he can't!"

"I find it funny I only just figured out who Fire-Eyes is." Solace gasped again. "Don't worry, brother. My body dies, but my soul..."

Solace held up his ring, and then he was gone.

LADY SHADE

THE BEAUTY AND MAGNIFICENCE OF BRONZEGLADE WAS NOW Milla's, by will of Eratta. His funeral would be tomorrow and he was going to be buried beside Teffly. Milla didn't mind that. The man had so much love in his heart that there was enough room for both of them.

Word had spread that spirit Solace Blue had returned to its ring, by the hands of Green-Eyes, and Fire-Eyes hadn't appeared during the murder. Milla remembered going to see Solace to understand the mind of the wolf, and he had been right. The mind of man in the wolf is what made a lycanthrope so dangerous.

Funny enough, the accusations which led to Eratta's death hadn't been far from the truth, and Milla was amazed she hadn't noticed it earlier. The lycanthrope that guarded Bronzeglade was older than any resident, so she searched the town's history and found her answer within records that had barely survived the fire.

"Father James Blossom, son of Oliver Blossom," she said.

A lycanthrope father and son. Oliver Blossom had a child despite being a priest, but guided his son James on lycanthropy. Taught him how to control it and how to fuse the human and wolf, in mind and soul. Blossom had been keen to be rid of the inquisitors and Milla, and had gotten angry because he feared for his life.

The first night she was attacked, when Green-Eyes had attacked her and Father Blossom had been the only person who'd known, Milla had assumed that Green-Eyes had smelled the silver, which was a common occurrence and was suggested in the journals that even in their human shape, the smell of silver was strong for lycanthropes. It had been used as a test for centuries.

Milla looked her revolver over. Six shots left.

"I'm guessing you figured it out, too." Tubiel walked up beside her.

"Father Blossom is Green-Eyes." Milla nodded. "Yeah, I did."

"You know, it's never as romantic as they say." Tubiel sighed. "Truths usually come in the silence."

"Yeah. I can at least kill one."

"As is the fate of hunters. Solace fixed up my arm before he returned to the ring, but I'm still pretty banged up." Tubiel held up the ring and the gem gleamed blue. "And now that I have it, I can see him and speak to him. He says you can confront Blossom in his church. He's alone there now. Question him and kill him."

"Such is the fate of a huntress." Milla gave a sad smile. "But if I'm honest, I've felt happiness in this town. With Eratta, with real friends like you and Uvire. Hell, avenging Eratta's death was the greatest hunt I've ever done."

"You have a fire in your heart." Tubiel shrugged. "But the truth is, it's the warm fire of a hearth and you've been letting it spread through your entire house."

"Since when were you one for spiritual advice?"

"I get it. I was the same."

Milla chuckled. "Now, for the hard part." She sighed and got up. "Thank you, Tubiel."

"Always." He nodded, with a smile.

The walk to the church was a heavy one and her heart was low. Father Blossom was a good man, and she didn't know if he deserved this. She beamed when she found herself cursing Eratta for softening her heart, but that quickly faded. She arrived at the market square sooner than expected and stared at the church, its gleaming white spire piercing the sky. Milla began traversing across the square and stopped in front of the church's small door. She opened it and stepped into the church, her footsteps echoing. Once she entered the heart of the church, she saw Father Blossom preparing a chalice of wine on the altar, dressed in white and green robes. He turned to face Milla, bowed his head and set the chalice down on the altar. Dark clouds washed the light from the windows and Blossom was cast in shadow. Then the light returned and he looked at her, with a confused expression.

"I have to ask," Milla said. "Why did you try to kill me?"

The light was dashed by the clouds once again, and Blossom's eyes glinted green in the dark. Then the light reappeared. He stared at the sky and red began to creep in. He pulled up his sleeves to reveal his silver bracers, then took a cloth and began cleaning the feet of a Jesus statue at the side of the altar.

"Why?" Milla asked.

"A huntress lingering on such questions." Blossom sighed. "If our Lord truly made you a huntress, I wouldn't be here, no?"

"Answer my question."

"Is self-preservation not an explanation?" Blossom looked to the window once again as the red continued to creep over the sky. "I'm assuming you know a few pieces of the puzzle. But understanding, no, you have none. I can see that."

"You aren't even looking at me!" she hissed.

Blossom whipped away the filthy cloth and plunged it into a bucket behind the altar. "I don't need to." He rinsed the dirt from the cloth.

Milla reached down to her holster and gripped her revolver.

"Go ahead. Shoot me." He took the wet cloth and moved on to the statue of Mary. "I can't defend myself. I haven't killed anyone."

"The moon's out."

"Full and beautiful, as are all God's creations. "You know, Miss Shade, I've been wondering about you. Who you are, your intentions. How much you knew about me. About yourself, even. About this town, lycanthropy. About the amber."

"Really?"

"Really." Blossom smiled. "Do you know who carried out the murder?"

"No." The huntress shrugged.

He finished cleaning the feet of Mary, rinsed off the cloth and left it in the water, then stood. Silence hung for a moment.

"Tubiel did," Blossom said. "Four nights later, I went after him. Nearly killed him, too, but the Golden Wolf was tougher than I thought. What makes it interesting was who he attacked. It took me a *long* time to find out who that was, but I eventually did."

"My mother. The only other surviving hunter of the Shade name."

Blossom appeared confused again. Miss Shade pointed her revolver at him as he looked her up and down. She was in a flowing black dress and her wrists glinted silver in the red light. He stepped back.

"You wrong," Fire-Eyes said. "It was me." She fired.

The bullet went through Blossom's shoulder. He staggered back, blood bursting from the wound. He spun and slammed chest-first into the marble floor.

Blossom hissed, pulling himself up the steps, and grappled with one of the silver bracers. "It's possession of your mind is so strong, Milla, that not even silver bracers can stop the beast." He gasped and managed to smile as he rolled onto his back to face her. "It's... it's saddening."

Fire-Eyes crouched, her red hair draping around her, eyes glinting orange in the light of dusk which shone through every window and casted the room in crimson. She pressed her revolver against the center of his forehead, glaring deep into his eyes.

"The best thing about lycanthropes isn't the wolf," Fire-Eyes said.

"It's the human. She makes the perfect huntress. Heartless, cunning, smart. Can kill anyone and anything. She manifested her humanity, at last."

"Bullshit." Blossom gasped. "I—"

"You, the protector. The guard dog of the flock, from the other wolves." Fire-Eyes smiled and pushed his head onto the marble.

The red light faded to black and the pair stood in a room lit only by starlight.

"Milla, can you hear me?" Blossom called out.

Fire-Eyes pulled the trigger. The shot echoed and someone outside shouted.

Milla stepped back, watching the blood from Blossom's head pool over the marble floor and down the steps. She darted her gaze down to the gun. Fire-Eyes clicked the safety off, and Milla clicked it back on and pointed it underneath her chin. Fire-Eyes thrashed her head. Then Milla held it still. She breathed in, smiled, and thought of Eratta waiting for her. With one chamber, she could kill two of the most powerful lycanthropes to ever live. Her little sister would inherit the estate and could get away from their father.

Yes, this was the answer to all her prayers.

Bang!

EPILOGUE
WIDOWED

It was a biting cold night and Nathaniel was sitting on a rock beside two graves, on the edge of the Bronzeglade. Errata was blood and soul of this land, and was buried beside Milla—a woman he'd truly loved. Nathaniel could tell in the way Errata talked, the way he smiled. She was a good woman. A strong person.

"You two didn't deserve this world." Nathaniel sighed and looked at Milla's grave. "Even you. I've forgiven you, you know. You probably died with some guilt in your heart, knowing what you'd done. That you kept it secret from me. But I saw it in your eyes. Eratta tried to keep secrets from me once, too."

An orange bird fluttered from the bare branches, above Nathaniel's head. It landed on a tree stump a few feet from him and chirped to the moon.

"Not your time to be awake, little thing." Nathaniel smiled. "Got to sleep."

The chirping bird flew back into the darkness of the trees.

"You were so good to me, Eratta." He shook his head. "You... you saved my life three times. You paid for me to live. Hardly worked me. Brought me to a land I loved. You didn't care about my past. Oh, if only the others knew they have a Frenchman in their midst. I suppose you understood, being a Dane and all. You let me bring my mother and had her nursed to health. And that's why I can forgive you, Milla. Because through it all, through your rage, you did it because you cared about the people around you. You hated our society because you thought it hurt us, and maybe you were right. I hope the two of you are happy up there. Hope you're together." Nathaniel stood and brushed the tears from his eyes.

He stopped. The wind whispered something in his ear and he turned to it. A sound through the trees, past the barren bark, across the glistening roots and rocks, beyond the darkness. He heard it again, louder this time.

Nathaniel smiled and sat back down. His mind loved playing tricks these days.

ABOUT THE AUTHOR

Ymir A. Lethe is a student who has been writing stories since the age of nine. They grew up reading the likes of Tolkien and Gemmell, but found much of their true inspiration in old stories such as Greek mythology, Irish folk tales, and urban legends.

They also love music—Gorillaz, Marilyn Manson, Imagine Dragons, Nirvana. If it's a band with four members or less, Ymir probably loves it.

Lightning Source UK Ltd.
Milton Keynes UK
UKHW011842230920
370426UK00005B/120